THE MOUNTIES ALWAYS GET
KNOW WHICH MAN TO GET . . .

. . . which isn't always so easy. T[...]
to Corporal Tim Shaver of the RC[...] as he [...]
the tangled skein of a plot to assassinate Russian Premier
Alexei Kosygin while the Kremlin's top man is on a state
visit to Vancouver. With the KGB, the CIA, the Canadian
Special Branch and a very expensive freelance hit-man
(specially imported from the States) involved, things are
likely to get pretty rough. And they do. By the time of this
high-tension thriller's shattering climax, Shaver has been
stomped, shot, drugged, and generally messed around too
much – *much* too much – for his health and peace of mind.
But by then he's also learned one hell of a lot about the
deadly art of Russian Roulette . . .

Also by Tom Ardies
in Panther Books

Their Man in the White House
This Suitcase is Going to Explode
Pandemic

Tom Ardies

Russian Roulette

Panther

Granada Publishing Limited
Published in 1975 by Panther Books Ltd
Frogmore, St Albans, Herts AL2 2NF

First published in Great Britain by Angus &
Robertson (UK) Ltd 1975 under the title *Kosygin is Coming.*
Copyright © 1974 by Tom Ardies
Made and printed in Great Britain by
Cox & Wyman Ltd
London, Reading and Fakenham
Set in Linotype Pilgrim

To E.T.S.

It's an ill wind that coughs blood.

– Old Polish proverb

One

They're never what you expect, Shaver thought, cap in hand. Petapiece had referred to himself as commander on the telephone, even though, by his own admission, he had surrendered that wartime rank some thirty years ago. So Shaver had pictured Petapiece as a very tiddly type, his clothes worn like a uniform, his affliction like a banner. He'd had it all quite settled in his mind's eye: ruddy complexion, severe haircut, stiff white mustache, briar pipe smelling unquestionably Navy. Tweed jacket with leather patch elbows. And – as the final touch – one sleeve empty, turned up, pinned.

Instead, as if purposely mocking Shaver's carefully structured fancies, the Vernon Prep school tie, Petapiece's idea of suitable identification, provided the only hint that here sat one of Her Majesty's faithful servants.

A poor start, Shaver decided. They hadn't even met and already he was disappointed. He stuffed his cap into his pocket and ventured farther into the dismal basement clubrooms and wondered what he was supposed to do now. The plan was for them to strike up a casual conversation and take it from there, but an appropriate opening line, for some reason, simply wouldn't come to mind. Shaver thought that it would be wildly funny if he stomped across to Petapiece's table and clicked his heels together and snapped off a smart salute. Corporal Timothy Shaver, one of the Royal Mounted's more able officers, reporting for duty as ordered, sirrah.

'Still pissing down?' Petapiece asked.

'Yes,' Shaver said, surprised at how easily this first hurdle had been met. One couldn't be lost for an answer to that question. It was always raining in October in Vancouver. Great lashing barrels of it, and a bone-chilling cold to boot.

No doubt that's why so many English came to settle and suffer. It reminded them of their equally miserable homeland. 'Bloody ridiculous.'

'Then I'll stay awhile,' Petapiece decided, puffy eyes flicking over the younger man. He twirled his glass and the inch of amber at the bottom turned to froth and he needed another drink.

'Let me buy,' Shaver offered. He took off his raincoat and shook it out and folded it carefully. Petapiece, he noted, was still wearing his, a crinkled rag with the waterproofing gone several seasons past, and a black ring around the collar. For an act, it was a pretty good one, Shaver thought grudgingly. Seedy and unkempt would be a kind description. Commander Petapiece needed many things to make him an acceptable drinking companion – and the first was a bath. 'The same?'

'McEwen's Pale.'

'Sounds fine.' Shaver deposited his coat in an empty chair, selected another for himself, and signaled to the bartender.

'They serve it properly? Warm?'

'You go get them,' Petapiece said softly. 'It's self-service here. You'll see why.'

Shaver nodded and got up. That had been stupid of him, he thought. These clubrooms were the social side of Headquarters, British Columbia Branch, Canadian War Amputees Association – or, as the members preferred it, The Stump Club.

'Pick up a couple of bags of chips, too, will you?' Petapiece asked. 'The kind with the imitation vinegar. The Bar-B-Q ones if they're out.'

'Right,' Shaver said, thinking that this was a bit much. Petapiece would be wanting garlic sausages and pickled eggs next, and all on his tab, no doubt. It was almost the end of the month, and a man in Petapiece's supposed circumstances, a poor pensioner sucking drinks, could hardly be expected to buy. The foxy bastard.

Shaver went to the bar and got the chips from their display rack, conscious of Petapiece's reflection in the mirror, smug and smiling, watching. A tasteless neon sign – THE AMP-

8

LIGHT ROOM, it proclaimed, flickering maddeningly – warned him that he ought to be careful. Petapiece had made out on the phone that he'd earned his club membership honorably, and yet, obviously, he was whole. What else would he lie about?

'One-eight-oh,' the bartender announced, ringing up the sale. His left arm had been cut off deep into the shoulder and he moved on stiff false legs. Shaver pushed back the two dimes in change and tried not to notice his gratitude.

'Don't mind if I do,' the bartender said. He dropped the coins in a cup under the bar and they clattered noisily. 'New here, aren't you?'

'Yes,' Shaver admitted. He could still hear one of the dimes rolling in the cup. There had been few previous donations, if any. 'First time.'

'I thought so,' the bartender said. He hesitated, considering something more, and then decided against it. But he did glance briefly at Petapiece's table and there had been the suggestion of a frown. A small show of concern for a young man fallen into bad company.

Shaver pretended not to notice that either and took his gifts to Petapiece. He was still rankled at having to buy, and it didn't help to tip when it wasn't expected, but he ought to keep up a brave front, he thought. There seemed to be something big in the wind and it was important to start out on the right foot with his new master. If his usual luck held – and why shouldn't it? – he'd be out of step soon enough.

'Good man,' Petapiece enthused, welcoming him back. He reached for the tray eagerly and took possession of both bags of chips. 'Did the barman give you any trouble?'

Shaver sat down and sampled the McEwen's. It was warm and good. 'No. Should he have?'

'Didn't I tell you?' Petapiece opened one of the cellophane bags with his yellow teeth and dumped the contents onto the terry-cloth tabletop. 'It's a private club. Members and their guests only. You'll have to join.'

'Can't I come as your guest?'

Petapiece's grubby fingers moved through the chips, picking the best for himself, leaving the culls for his benefactor. 'I'd prefer not. For obvious reasons.'

9

'Then why don't we meet someplace else?'

'You can charge it to your expense account,' Petapiece said, trying hard not to sound patronizing. 'I'm certain no one will question you. It's a perfectly legitimate expense.'

Shaver regarded him unsurely. McDermott would never allow such a thing in CIB. But then it was bound to be cushy at Special Branch. They could even afford disguises there. 'How much?'

'Fifteen dollars.'

'Fifteen?' Shaver echoed, flushing slightly. He had sounded like a complaining mouse.

'It's for a full year.'

Shaver took a better look around and found nothing to change his first impression of the club's gloomy basement rooms. The place had no warmth or style or dignity or anything else to commend it. There were only three other patrons, two old men arguing near the unused shuffleboard, and a Yul Brynner type with a shaved head, sporting the empty sleeve he had conjured up for Petapiece, playing darts by himself. The card room at the rear was empty.

Shaver decided that it was an altogether dreary establishment and that he would not come again except in the line of duty. If he was running a counterespionage network, he'd establish his control someplace slightly more spiffy, he thought. The Hotel Van's Timber Club. Or perhaps the Georgia lounge.

'That's associate membership, of course,' Petapiece was saying. 'If you could arrange the loss of a limb, you'd be eligible for the regular rate, which would mean a saving of five dollars.' He crunched lovingly on a chip. 'That's assuming you're a veteran?'

'Yes,' Shaver said, wondering if this deviousness was a part of the man's nature. Petapiece would have read his file – and his service record along with it – before considering him for any sort of assignment with Special Branch. 'Air Force. Korean Conflict. Commendation Ribbon. I rose through the Ranks to Airman Second Class.'

'Really?' Petapiece said. He finished the chips to his satisfaction, wiped his fingers on his raincoat, and picked up the second package. 'What was the commendation for?'

'A management-improvement suggestion.'

'Ah,' Petapiece exclaimed, laughing for the first time. 'Then this trouble with McDermott, it isn't your first brush with authority, eh? You've always been a trouble-maker?'

'I'm afraid so,' Shaver said, and he thought that if the admission bothered him, Petapiece hid it well. The laughter continued, rising an octave, and then slowly dwindled away, dying of natural causes, not from his heroics.

'Pick up a club application form on the way out,' Petapiece instructed. 'If you can't find a member to recommend you, forge a name . . .' He tore open the second bag and the chips spilled out and he unearthed the largest and popped it into his mouth. 'It's an accepted practice here. The Liquor Control Board couldn't care less. All it asks is the appearance of legitimacy.'

'Couldn't you recommend me?'

'Hardly,' Petapiece answered, frowning. 'I don't know you that well.'

Ha, ha, Shaver thought. He retreated to his ale and watched covertly as Petapiece foraged through the pile of chips. Until now, he'd been rather pleased and proud with the idea of an assignment, however temporary, to Special Branch. But this son of a bitch was doing his best to ruin things. He'd be further ahead transferring to the Musical Ride.

I'll manage, Shaver was going to say, or something equally childish, but fortunately the urge passed. They sat in silence until nothing remained of sufficient quality for Petapiece's exacting palate. Then, finally finished, he pushed the crumbs aside, added a few more smears to his raincoat, and patted around half-heartedly for a plainly non-existent cigarette.

'Have one of mine,' Shaver said at last, producing a pouch of Sweet Caps.

'Oh,' Petapiece said, as if surprised by this generosity. 'Much obliged . . .' His expression changed as he saw what was being offered. 'No filters, eh?'

'No,' Shaver took one for himself and started to return the pouch, but a grimy hand came up, stopping him.

'Beggars,' Petapiece grinned. He snaked one free, licked an end, and carefully committed it to his mouth.

Shaver lit the cigarette for him, and then his own, and then there was another silence, longer this time. If the grubby mooch wants to be difficult, it's a game two can play, Shaver thought. He'd come to this meeting with good intentions – eagerly, in fact, because he wanted out from under McDermott, and this looked like the chance – but that didn't mean he was inclined to kiss ass.

'Did you see the morning paper?' Petapiece asked then, sensing his mood. 'We seem to be getting awfully cozy with Moscow. Premier Kosygin's coming over for a state visit.'

Shaver nodded and pretended an interest in the dart player. It struck him that the poor fellow must have been left-handed originally. He was still trying to get his double to start.

'It's what brings us together here today.'

'Oh?' Shaver said. 'How dull . . .' That was twaddle, and must sound like it, he thought, immediately sorry. Nothing was ever dull when it involved the Russians. But he couldn't back down now. 'Guard duty is a little out of my line.'

'Don't turn silly on me,' Petapiece complained. 'It doesn't suit you, and I've got no time for it, frankly. I'd just as soon send you marching back to McDermott.'

Shaver tried to look properly cringing. 'Oh, please, sar. Don' do tha'. I ha' too much money invested.'

Petapiece blinked at him through the smoke, his pale blue eyes oddly expressionless, his mouth a stiff line, and for a while Shaver wasn't sure which way it might go. But at last the laughter came and he was more relieved than he would want to admit. There had been something of the wild animal lurking in those cold eyes; the suggestion of a leashed animal; the savagery barely restrained. Shaver thought once more that he ought to be careful of the man. Commander Petapiece, he decided, would always be among the hunters, not the hunted.

'Brassy bugger, aren't you?' Petapiece asked, but it wasn't a question. 'No wonder McDermott had you suspended.' He laughed again, louder this time, and it carried across the room, causing the dart player to look around, and the old men paused in their argument, like dogs alerted by an alien sound.

Shaver shrugged and let it go at that. The lust for victory had long since left him and he was quite happy to settle for a draw. 'How's your drink?' he asked.

'The other wing,' Petapiece agreed.

When Shaver returned, there was a new pocketbook, a soft black pigskin, sitting in the middle of the table. It was much too expensive for the character that Petapiece was portraying, so it must belong to him, Shaver surmised. He put the drinks down and picked the thing up and put his change inside and took careful note of the wad of new bills. There must be several hundred dollars if there was a penny. Special Branch really didn't scrimp.

'That'll keep you going for a few days,' Petapiece said. 'If you need more, you can always find me here, and all you've got to do is ask.' He took a long pull on his drink and wiped his mouth on his sleeve. 'Within reason, of course.'

Shaver was a bit taken aback. He frankly had been surprised to get such a large advance at all, for that matter. In the CIB, you paid your expenses out of your own pocket, settling up with them later, and you were lucky if you came out even. But then Petapiece would be aware that he'd been suspended without pay and that it had been almost a month since his last check. 'Who do I kill?'

'Oh, I don't think it will come to that,' Petapiece answered softly. 'I imagine a simple kidnaping will prove quite sufficient. There's no need going overboard.'

Shaver lowered his voice to the merest whisper. 'Kidnaping . . .?'

'Meet your victim,' Petapiece said, tapping the pocketbook. 'Mr. Rudolph Henke. You ought to strike it off quite well together. He's also got a reputation as a troublemaker.'

Shaver flipped through his new possession until he came to a color photograph in one of the plastic inserts.

Petapiece was still softly talking. '. . . a refugee from the Russian excesses in Latvia. Tried the United States first and then decided he'd rather be a Canadian. Been here eight years all told. Five as a landed immigrant. The last three as a full citizen.'

Shaver stared at the photograph and decided that the kidnaping remark was a joke. He'd heard a lot of wild stories about Special Branch, but they kept their noses clean, all the same. Not like the crazy Americans.

'Think you could take him?'

'Sure,' Shaver said, going along with the gag, and he thought that there'd be no trouble locating him, either. Henke had a unique face. It was as round as a ball, a perfect circle, almost, and set off by very prominent ears, sticking out like handles on a jug. Horn-rimmed glasses, a deeply furrowed brow, and a protruding underlip combined to give him a faintly quizzical appearance, hinting at some low form of intelligence, but the effect was spoiled by the wide pug nose. He'd be in his late forties, Shaver judged, his close-cropped hair thinning, his chin barely discernible in the loose folds of fat at his throat.

'A very dangerous man,' Shaver said, not knowing what else to say, but thinking that some further comment was required. He closed the pocketbook and slipped it into his coat.

Petapiece nodded solemnly. 'The Russians think so. They figure him as a potential assassin.'

Shaver couldn't help laughing. 'This dear little flower? A threat to Kosygin?'

'Seriously,' Petapiece said, his annoyance growing. 'Henke's the top man on the KGB surveillance list drawn up for Kosygin's visit. They want Henke out of circulation the whole time Kosygin is in Canada.'

'The whole time?' Shaver repeated dumbly. He wished he had read the morning paper more carefully. All he could recall was that the visit was to begin sometime next week, and that the first stop, after Ottawa, was to be in Vancouver.

'That's right,' Petapiece said. 'The full eight days. It's not just here that the KGB thinks Henke might try something. They're worried he might make his move anywhere on the tour.'

'Well,' Shaver said slowly, the light dawning, 'that makes

it difficult, doesn't it? Especially if Henke has good connections?'

Petapiece's solemn nod came again. 'The best. He's one of those professional protesters and a darling of the Civil Liberties Union. They've gone to bat for him at least half a dozen times.'

Ah, yes, Shaver thought. The light dawns and the plot it thickens. This explained why he'd been chosen for the job. They needed somebody under suspension, with his hearing coming up shortly, and with a fair-to-middle chance of getting the sack. Somebody desperate enough to stick his neck out. 'What you're saying is that the usual thing won't work?'

'I'm afraid not,' Petapiece admitted. 'Eight days is too long a pull for us to try any sort of trumped-up criminal charge. The Civil Liberties Union would cream us if we tried that route. They'd have Henke bailed out next morning on anything less than a murder charge.'

Shaver turned away to watch the dart player. He had the angry feeling that he had been unfairly trapped. He hadn't taken the job, and he had every right to refuse something quite this stupid, but his acceptance was somehow being treated as a foregone conclusion. 'Why doesn't somebody tell the Russians that our system doesn't provide for preventive detention?'

'Somebody has,' Petapiece replied mildly, 'but it didn't make much of an impression, apparently. The KGB boys were most insistent: Ottawa's assurance that Henke would be safely out of the way for the duration – or no visit.'

'An assurance that has been given?'

'What do you think? You saw the paper. The visit's on.'

'Of course,' Shaver said. 'Puddle-headed of me . . .' The last dart thudded into the board, and, like the others, it was far, far from its mark. He turned back to face Petapiece. It was a stupid question, but he ought to mention it anyway, Shaver thought, if only to hear how Petapiece fielded it. 'Why pick on me?'

'The powers-that-be thought you'd appreciate a chance to redeem yourself,' Petapiece said. 'Handle this properly and the outcome of your hearing is a foregone conclusion.' He spread open his hands on the table in a gesture of hopelessness. 'Mess it up . . .'

Sure, Shaver thought. Or refuse to take it on. He stared moodily into the unfathomable depths of his drink. This was quite a price to pay for bopping a superior officer on the nose. Especially when he deserved it. 'What did you have in mind?' he asked at last.

'Well,' Petapiece said. 'I'd hoped that would be apparent by now. Your job is to see that this Henke is indeed taken out of circulation.'

'Plain enough,' Shaver agreed. 'But that wasn't the question.' He thought bitterly that the thing really had been settled without even the courtesy of a discussion. *Your job*, the grubby mooch had said, sounding so goddam superior, and about as subtle as a cocked gun. 'I meant to ask how.'

'Your problem,' was the answer. 'McDermott may hate your guts, but he speaks highly of your resourcefulness. I thought I'd leave it entirely up to you.'

'Pig's eye,' Shaver said. 'You mean I'm strictly on my own? No help whatsoever at all?'

'You said you could handle him alone.'

Like hell, Shaver thought. Now the man was putting words into his mouth. He'd said no such thing.

'You know the old saw about too many cooks,' Petapiece said. 'It also applies to cops. You can start stumbling over each other on this kind of job. So it's much safer to use just one man.'

Shaver wondered why Petapiece should persist in his deviousness. Surely there was no need for lies at this stage. 'Especially if his connection with the force is tenuous at best?'

Petapiece hesitated for only a moment. 'Whatever made you think you're still on the force?'

'I'm not?' Shaver asked unsurely.

'Your connection, at the moment, is non-existent,' Petapiece said. 'According to your personnel file, your hearing has already been held, and it went rather badly for you, I fear. Dishonorable discharge.'

Shaver sat staring at him in disbelief.

'Rogue cop, you are,' Petapiece said, inordinately pleased

with himself. 'You've been booted out on your arse and the force can hardly be responsible for any more of your mischief. But that's only a temporary state of affairs. You'll be back in good grace soon enough.'

This is unreal, Shaver thought. First the bullying, and now this, for God's sake. He'd had the buck passed his way many times – one of the occupational hazards of police work – but this was the first time anyone had ever asked for change. 'Just so long as the force's good name isn't blemished?'

Petapiece managed a small smile. 'That's it.'

Shaver struggled against the anger mounting in him. He'd been screwed, plain and simple, and nothing could change that, no matter how loudly he screamed. Either he took the job or he sat back and watched fifteen years' service go down the drain.

'You're sure this is as easy as you say?' he asked careful not to commit himself completely. He wanted to make certain there were no more surprises. Such as Henke being a black belt in judo.

'It ought to be a piece of cake,' Petapiece assured him. 'Henke's a bachelor. Lives alone in the West End. No girl or any particularly close friends.'

Shaver was immediately on the alert. 'Queer?'

'I don't think so. There's nothing in his file to suggest that. Just because a chap doesn't want a woman nagging him.'

Shaver thought Petapiece sounded a trifle too defensive. 'Perhaps I ought to have a look at his file.'

'No,' Petapiece said. 'There's no need for that. I don't want you showing your mug back at headquarters until this is over. I know all you have to know – and the main thing is that Henke's got good cause for hating the Russians.'

'How's that?'

'His family. Wiped out.'

How nice, Shaver thought. So the poor bastard comes here, where a man's claimed safe from oppression from sea to shining sea, and what the hell do we do to him? Shaver told himself he ought to advise Petapiece to get stuffed. He ought to bop him on the nose, too, just like McDermott, and make the supposed discharge honest. He really ought to do that, he thought, staring into his drink, but he knew he wouldn't. He was more concerned for his own neck than he'd ever be for Henke's. 'What day did you have in mind?' he asked.

Petapiece glanced at the calendar behind the bar. 'Kosygin arrives next Wednesday. So let's say you grab Henke by Monday at the latest. That gives you four full days to prepare.'

'You don't mind before that?'

'No. The sooner the better.'

Exactly, Shaver thought. If he waited too long, the Russians might get nervous, and he didn't want them on his back. That could lead to real trouble. On the other hand, if he made the snatch too early, the Civil Liberties union would have that much more time to sniff around, and he didn't want some bright young lawyer connecting Henke's disappearance with Kosygin's impending arrival. He wouldn't earn any Brownie points if someone made that connection and started screaming police state. Shaver thought of raising this question and then decided against it. Petapiece had suggested Monday when first asked his preference. Monday was middle ground, not too soon, and not too late. Monday was best.

'All right,' Shaver said, tired of bucking the inevitable. 'You've got a deal. Consider it done.' The words were no sooner out than he regretted them, but what choice had he, really? One must rise to the occasion. He finished his McEwen's – the afternoon's only compensation – and leaned back in his chair and let himself go limp. 'Another for the road?'

'Why not?' Petapiece asked, wetting his lips, but he made no move to get it.

Sweet Mary Mother of Jesus, Shaver thought, pushing up wearily. 'Let me buy,' he said.

Two

Rudolph Henke was a creature of habit. Though the sounds of traffic awakened him by seven o'clock, he would remain in bed for at least another hour, his eyes closed and his mind shut tight, until the pain in his bladder became unbearable. Then he would struggle out of bed and cross blindly to the toilet to relieve himself and he would vow that tomorrow would be different. He'd promise himself to get out of bed the moment the pain started. But the next morning the same thing would happen. The routine was set. It never changed.

Few things ever did for Henke. He had a pattern and he stuck to it. He read the morning paper, thoroughly, from back to front, while eating a breakfast which invariably consisted of instant coffee, a boiled egg, and two slices of toast. If he was behind schedule, he sometimes skipped the Classified but never the Personal. They were must reading. Inviolate. People bared their souls there – *Ted. Will fast till contacted. Phone John. No questions asked.*–and Henke took a perverse pleasure in the sexual frustrations of others. His own were gargantuan.

When he finished with the paper, Henke turned on his portable radio and took it into the bathroom with him, switching back and forth among the morning talk shows while he performed his ritual toilet. He brushed his teeth first, and then he shaved, and then he had a long hot bath, trying to decide which was the main 'issue of the day' on the talk shows.

Once this was settled, usually by eleven o'clock, Henke turned to CHQM, 'the good music station,' and listened to its offerings while he got dressed. Though it was not meant to, the music had a lulling effect on him and he often found himself rushing desperately in order to catch the noon trolley bus downtown.

Henke boarded the trolley at the Stanley Park turnaround and transferred to a Macdonald bus at Pender and Burrard. He got off at Robsonstrasse and had two beers and a pork meat pie in the beer parlor at the Rembrandt Hotel. He discouraged company at his table by talking earnestly to himself and by catching and pretending to eat flies.

The next stop was the Public Library. On the average of two or three times a month a man he knew only as Donaldson would join him at his table in the Periodicals Section. Donaldson would give him some job to do – an assignment, Donaldson called it, trying to sound important – and then the routine would be broken until the thing was done. Normally it didn't take more than one evening.

If he didn't get a job, and it was only on rare occasions that he did, Henke had the day to himself, to spend as he pleased. If the talk shows had a good 'issue' going – with the maniac fringe really fired up and taking to the streets – he'd sometimes join in the protest. The subject didn't particularly matter. Since September he had protested alleged police brutality in Gastown, the plans to demolish Christ Church Cathedral, and the renewed American bombing of Hanoi and Haiphong. He was especially fond of demonstrations at the American Embassy in the Burrard Building. The CBC's television studios were just down the street and one could always be assured that the news cameras would be grinding away. He'd made the six o'clock news last time. On the screen a full twenty seconds. Marvelous.

If he couldn't find anything suitable to protest, Henke usually spent the afternoon in the library, or – if there was a film he hadn't seen – at one of the porno movie houses on Granville. At the library his tastes were divided between erotica and technical data on the various means of decimating mankind. He was especially high on viruses, ranked nerve gases second, and placed nuclear weapons a poor third. He felt quite strongly that facilities should remain intact.

Henke left the library about four o'clock and had two more glasses of beer at the Rembrandt. He stopped along

Robsonstrasse, patronizing the same merchants, and then if it wasn't raining heavily, he walked back to his rooming house. At this hour the streets were full of working girls headed home to their apartments in the West End. He'd pick one going his way and follow a few steps behind her and imagine himself doing certain sexual things to her. If there was a heavy rain, he'd retrace his route of the morning, using two buses to get back to the turnaround at Stanley Park. Only rarely did he use a taxi.

Henke switched from beer to rye whiskey when he got home. He had two or three drinks while he watched the television news programs, changing back and forth between the various stations, including those in Seattle. He wanted to see the films of as many demonstrations as possible. They were very educational.

When the last news program ended at seven o'clock, Henke opened a bottle of wine and began preparing his dinner, sipping directly from the bottle as he went about his labors. He always tried to fix himself a decent evening meal, providing his routine wasn't broken by a protest rally, or an assignment from the man he knew only as Donaldson. He had a theory that if one ate well it didn't matter how much one drank and as a result he lavished a great deal of time and attention on his dinner menus.

Still a pattern persisted. He had the same cuts of meat Sunday through Wednesday, and then something exotic – such as hare – on Thursday. He ate fish Friday, not out of religious considerations, but simply because that seemed the most appropriate day, historically, and some sort of fowl on Saturday. He enjoyed nothing better than a nice, fat goose.

Henke dined alone – there had never been a guest in his flat – and finished the bottle of wine with the meal. Then he got out the rye whiskey again and had a couple of straight shots while he washed the dishes and two or three more while he thumbed through the evening newspaper. Having been so thorough in the morning, he was selective now, skipping through the headlines for totally new developments and making sure to read only the editorials, the letters to the editor, and a few favorite columnists. By the time he finished, his eyes wouldn't be focusing properly, and there would be a familiar ache deep in his right temple. He'd toss the paper aside and turn on the television again and stare blindly at the screen for a while, hardly conscious of the program, and not really caring. You're drunk, he would tell himself after a while, and he would struggle to his feet, the world swirling about him, and he would somehow manage to stagger to the bedroom, pulling off his clothes as he went. It was open to argument whether he fell asleep or passed out when he sprawled on the bed.

The same things would happen day after day after day. Rudolph Henke was a creature of habit. There was a definite pattern to his life. A fixed routine.

Shaver finished his coffee and looked at his watch. It was time to commit suicide. He paid the waitress and turned up his collar and braced himself before pushing outside. An arctic front had brought an abrupt overnight change in the weather. The sky was clear and an icy wind was blowing off Lost Lagoon.

Just my luck, Shaver thought. Blue balls coming up. He hunched into the wind and crossed the street and picked his way down the concrete steps leading into the trolley-bus turnaround. He thought again that he was stupid to try anything quite this crazy – but a sleepless night hadn't produced any other solution.

Shaver had spent two days, Thursday and Friday, trailing Henke, and never once had he seen the opportunity for a decent kidnaping. How could there be? No way, Shaver thought. The lazy pig didn't venture out until noon and he was home again before dark. He rode the bus and went to the library, the pub, and a few small shops. Broad daylight and people everywhere.

And Henke's flat? Well, that was a flipping fortress, wasn't it? The attic of an old rooming house crammed with other tenants. Two flights of stairs to drag the lop-eared bastard down. Half a dozen doors to pass.

No, Shaver thought. That wouldn't do either. Much, much too risky. The only way was this way. He walked across the turnaround to where the old man and the trolley driver were sharing a bench overlooking the lagoon.

22

'Remember me?' Shaver asked.

'Sure,' the old man said.

'I said I'd be back.'

'Yes.'

Shaver sat down to the old man's left on the far side of the bench from the trolley driver. The old man remained very still – the slightest movement might betray his presence to the wind's probing fingers – and ignored the tear clinging precariously to his cheek. He must be senile, Shaver thought, full of self-reproach, and only a low-lifer would take advantage.

'You still want to do it?' Shaver asked.

'Why not?' the old man said.

Why not indeed? Shaver thought, his spirits rising. He wished that Petapiece could be present for this demonstration of resourcefulness. The commander would appreciate its pure subtlety. He'd realize it could only lead to hunter and prey becoming the best of friends.

'I ought to have your name first,' Shaver said, getting out his notebook.

'Harry,' the old man said.

'Harry,' Shaver repeated. He wrote that down. 'Have you got a last name?'

'Sure,' the old man said.

Henke switched the dial on his portable radio back to Jack Webster on CJOR. He liked Webster best of all the talk-show hosts. Old Blather McHaggis was a real shit-disturber. He got the maniac fringe worked up better than anyone else.

There was a woman on the hot line now. She had a high, squeaky voice, and she was talking so fast it was difficult to understand her.

Henke stopped toweling himself and leaned closer. What was she complaining about? Excrement?

Yes, that was it. Animal excrement. You couldn't go anywhere anymore without stepping in animal excrement. Sidewalks, boulevards, parks, lawns. All covered with animal excrement.

She's right, Henke thought. Take all those pigeons crapping under the eaves of this place. Right outside his window there were more deposits than the Royal Bank could boast.

Henke listened to the woman's screeching for a couple of minutes and then shrugged and switched to the soothing music of CHQM. It was no use monitoring the talk shows any longer. There simply wasn't a good 'issue' around today. But that was typical of a Saturday. It was always slow on a Saturday.

Something might develop, though, out of that news report from up island, where a construction worker had claimed that Omaha Mining had filled in a beaver pond and killed the beavers. What a classic case that presented. The very symbol of Canada ground under by American boots. If this was confirmed, the Yankee-baiters would be in full cry, and that might lead to another go at the American Embassy. Henke hoped it would come to that. It was time he tossed a few bricks for the benefit of the television cameras. He hadn't been in jail since July.

'The guy in the fur cap?' the old man said. 'He's one of the regulars around here. You could set your clock by him.'

Shaver glanced absently at his watch. It was getting on toward noon, and yesterday the fur cap had shown up about eleven, and the day before not at all. So much for his informant's accuracy. 'What category?' Shaver asked.

'Strictly a dumper,' the old man said, and it was obvious he was guessing. 'You watch him now. You'll see.'

The new arrival pulled a crumpled paper bag from his overcoat pocket and shuffled down to the water's edge. He moved in slow motion, progressing but a few inches with each step, sliding his feet forward rather than lifting them off the ground. Lame, Shaver had thought initially, but it was not that, only loose rubbers.

'Let me get this straight,' Shaver said, checking his list. 'You say there are the three methods? – piecemeal, scatter, and dump?'

'*Main* methods,' the old man corrected. 'The most popular. There must be a dozen variations. I would hesitate to attempt an accurate count.

'The most popular, then,' Shaver said, chastised. 'Piece-

24

meal is when you toss one crust at a time to your favorite? Scatter is when you fling a handful out in an arc so they all get a fair chance? And dump is when you throw it down in a pile and cause a wild scramble?'

'That's correct. Down in one big lump and watch the dogfight. Freud would have had a field day here.'

'Hold it,' Shaver said. 'Let me get that . . .' He turned the page of his notebook. 'You're suggesting that these are personality traits?'

'What else? When are we ever so naked as in our charity?'

Farther along the bench, the trolley driver cocked an eyebrow, regarded them both unsurely, and then returned undecided to his newspaper. Shaver was reminded that it was almost time to leave and still there was no sign of Henke. 'That's very interesting,' he said, writing it down.

The new arrival opened his bag and removed a single crust and called to the swans. They kept their distance, grandly indifferent, but the ducks rushed forward, complaining vociferously at his favoritism, and one was so indignant as to snap at his pant leg.

'The mallards,' the old man said, brushing over his error, 'are the ones with the green heads. That's the male. The dull brown ones are the females. It's very strange – the male is the colorful one in the animal world and it's inverse in man.'

'What about the blacks?'

'I used to shoot them before I got this bum leg,' the old man mused. 'Now I come down and feed them. Man is just as inconsistent as nature.'

'Isn't he?' Shaver agreed. He swore softly to himself. Where in hell was the lop-eared bastard?

Henke pulled his door shut and clattered down the steps. On the second-floor landing, as if on signal, a slim crack appeared at Number Six, and two pairs of eyes stared out at him.

'Good morning, Mendelssohn,' Henke said, brushing by. 'You, too, Wilbur.' He quickened his pace along the hall. 'You fellows must be happy. Just two more box tops and you'll have your Dick Tracy Detective Kit.'

There was a sharp clicking sound in answer. Henke smiled to himself and turned down into the first-floor stairwell. When he first moved in, he had been annoyed at the constant surveillance, but then he realized that it was to his advantage. It was as good as having a dog, and no food to buy, either.

An enormous woman with a glistening face stood in an open doorway at the bottom of the stairs. She was wearing a cap made of an old nylon stocking and a tattered housecoat purchased when she was perhaps half a dozen sizes smaller. There was a pink mule on one foot and a heavy blue ankle sock on the other.

'Mrs. Goldfarb,' Henke said, not breaking stride, 'expecting company, are you?' He was smiling again as he went out the front door. 'Or perhaps you've mistaken the date? It's tomorrow that you wear your Sunday best.'

The reply was lost in the slamming of the door. Dogs, Henke thought. As good as having dogs. He pulled his scarf around his throat – it was much colder than he had expected – and hurried down the front steps. That was the noon whistle. He was late as usual. He'd have to run.

The trolley driver folded his newspaper and dug into his vest pocket. Shaver waited for him to confirm the time and then rose as he did. 'You've been most helpful,' Shaver told the old man. 'How can I ever thank you?'

'The blacks are coots,' the old man said, seeming not to hear. 'A diving duck, not much thought of as a main dish for a meal, but as a broken field runner he sure can cover the ground. He's got to or else he'll lose his bread to the gulls.'

The driver was already halfway to the bus. Shaver turned to follow him. 'I really must go.'

'Gulls are the worst for chasing. They are the damndest bullies. Mean devils.'

'Really,' Shaver insisted.

'All right,' the old man said, defeated. He brushed away the tear clinging to his cheek. 'When will the article appear?'

'Next week sometime.'

'Will there be photographs?'

26

'Yes.'

'Wait,' the old man called. 'I don't get the paper. Will you bring me a copy?'

'I will,' Shaver lied. He dashed madly for the bus and squeezed aboard just as the doors were closing.

The driver looked at Shaver sourly as he fumbled with his change purse. 'I've got a schedule to keep,' he complained.

'You've got another passenger,' Shaver panted. 'See? He's coming down the hill now ...' He dropped a coin and bent to search for it. 'Surely you wouldn't leave him? It's twenty minutes till the next car.'

'The wait will do him good. Teach him a lesson.'

'One of your regulars?' Shaver asked softly, depositing his fare. 'Admit it now. You could set your clock by him.'

The driver's face softened. He was not a mean man. He just wanted to assert his authority. 'I couldn't help over-hearing out there. I take it you're a journalist?'

'If that's an unemployed reporter,' Shaver said cheerfully. He took the first seat beside the door and tucked his feet under against the heater. 'What did you think of that old gaffer?'

'He's certainly full of it, isn't he?' the driver laughed. 'You could fill a page with him and still have lots to spare.' He waited for the desperate knock before choosing to open the door. 'You say you're not employed. A freelancer, you mean?'

Shaver nodded and smiled hello to Henke. He lurched aboard, his breath coming in heavy gasps, and flung himself into the seat across the aisle. One soft hand made a fluttering motion toward the fare box. He would pay later.

'My wife's sister did some writing,' the driver said, start-ing up. 'Starved to death ...' He examined Shaver carefully in his mirror. 'And your dish also rattles, eh?'

'I have known better times,' Shaver admitted.

'My stomach could not stand the suspense,' the driver confided. 'The best thing about a steady job is the steady paycheck.' He looked at his watch and the bus picked up speed. 'What are you going to call this masterpiece?'

'No wise quacks, please,' Shaver told him, smiling once

more for Henke. '*The Gentle Art of Feeding Ducks*. But the editors will change it. They always do.'

'For a magazine?'

'No. Just one of the local papers.'

'Which one?'

'The *Sun*. I hope.'

The bus stopped and a youngish woman with an unhappy face got aboard. She wore no make-up, and her hair was done up in giant curlers, and her knees brushed together as she walked. From Mars, obviously, Shaver thought. He watched her walk to the rear and then turned back to the driver. 'I'm trying to get a steady job there. It's on account of my name. I'll be Brown from the *Sun*.'

'Excuse me,' Henke murmured. He stood up unsurely and paid his fare and quickly returned to his seat.

The driver went on for another half a block and then was suddenly overcome. 'Oh,' he cried, recovering just in time to avoid disaster. 'That's royal. My wife will enjoy that . . .' He peeked around his curtain and beamed at Henke. 'Get it? Brown from the *Sun*?'

'I got it,' Henke said, staring at Shaver with dull, flat eyes. It was their first close contact and it struck Shaver that the photograph Petapiece had provided was quite flattering. Henke was an ugly man, really, aged far beyond his years, and still blowing from his downhill run.

'Your article,' the driver burbled. 'I don't want to miss that. When will it appear?'

'It's not definite,' Shaver said, staring back. He actually should submit one. Everybody was asking. 'Perhaps a week Friday. The Leisure Section.'

The bus stopped again and picked up several more passengers. A withered old lady, a pinch-faced postman, a tormented mother heavy with yet another unwanted child. They trooped back to join the visitor from outer space.

Shaver found the flat eyes still challenging him when the procession had passed. 'You write about the feeding of ducks?'

'Why not?' Shaver demanded. 'If it means feeding myself . . .' He stopped and waited for his supposed anger to subside. 'It's a temporary measure only. I'm new here and must establish myself.'

'From where?'

'From Toronto.'

'Oh yes,' Henke said. 'Toronto. I've been there. It's a good place to be from.'

'I get it,' Shaver said, and the driver had another of his fits.

The bus continued downtown, more slowly now in the increasing traffic, taking on larger groups at each successive stop, and their jostling passage in the aisle made further conversation impossible. Shaver could see his grand plan crumbling, and it had been so wonderfully simple and direct, too. Strike up a friendship with his prey, buy him a beer or two, butter him up a bit, and then let it drop that their radical views coincided. Luring him to some private reckoning would have been a cinch after that. Don't all conspirators like to sneak off by themselves?

It was worth one more try, Shaver thought. He surrendered his seat to a matron and in the confusion of their exchange he managed to end up holding the handrail above Henke. 'I was a political writer in Toronto,' he began defensively. 'Specializing in exposés. You've heard of the Grenier Affair? The Vironde Scandal?'

'Vaguely.'

'I broke both those bastards,' Shaver said. 'Nailed them to the cross. Among others.' He lowered his voice confidentially. 'More than one cabinet minister has trembled at my pen.'

The man standing next to him edged away in alarm. The expression on his face made it clear what he was thinking. That's always been the trouble with the bus. You can't pick your company.

'Some reputation, by the sound of it,' Henke said, smiling. 'Why would you leave?'

'Leave?' Shaver scoffed. 'Dismissed, you mean. I was with the *Telegram*. More than a thousand jobs lost the day it folded.'

'But a man of your abilities? Surely one of the other papers there would take you on?'

'Me?' Shaver said, voice rising once more. 'I was too much the fascist for those other pinko rags. The first thing they want to see is your Communist Party membership card.' He turned on the man standing next to him. 'I'm reduced to ducks.'

'In this town?' Henke said, glancing out the window. 'You're just not trying hard enough. I myself could tell you of a good scandal right now. What would you say to that?'

'Ha.'

'It's true,' Henke said. He waited for the bus to stop and then got to his feet. 'You think this is a free country? It's a police state ...' He leaned forward until Shaver could feel his hot breath. 'I am persecuted. My every footstep hounded. Even now one of their agents follows me.'

'You are followed? By whom?'

'By you, pig,' Henke shrilled, and he spit in Shaver's face and plunged out the door.

The driver looked after him in astonishment. 'Is he mad?'

No, Shaver thought, wiping away the spittle. He's just smart, that's all. Too smart for his own good.

Three

First Voice: '. . . missionaries. Would you be interested in one of our church publications?'

Second Voice: 'I am not interested.'

First Voice: 'Well, are you interested in world peace?'

Second Voice: 'No. I am a munitions manufacturer.'

Shaver's watch, when he found it, hidden in his shoe, wasn't very helpful. The hands were at twelve and in his state that could mean midnight or noon. Midnight, most likely, he decided, his head throbbing. No one would dare hammer a door that aggressively on the prescribed day of rest.

Bogna came by the bed and went into the bathroom. 'You live?' she asked.

'Yes,' Shaver decided. 'My enemies stand stunned. Foiled again . . .' He closed his eyes against the pain. 'What was that all about?'

'The usual sadists.'

'Them,' Shaver said, the scraps of conversation finally registering. That settled one thing. Another day had begun.

'Why do they persist?'

'It's their religion.'

'To wake me at noon?'

'No. To wake you at ten. They came earlier but I refused to answer.'

'You are a woman of exceedingly sound judgment,' Shaver said solemnly.

'Oh?' Bogna said, her tone changing abruptly. 'Then why are you in my bed?'

The bathroom door slammed and the shower hit the tub. Shaver listened to its drum, to the squeak of her feet, and, after a minute or so, to the sound of her softly singing. Good, he thought, smiling despite the pain, and he got up and went into the kitchen to see if he had been intelligent enough to put aside an antidote.

The kitchen was a mess. The dinner dishes, not even scraped, lay slatternly in the sink, and the condiments were still on the table. Shaver shook his head. Ah, yes. You're quite the lady's man, aren't you, chum? Here's your evidence. Eat and run – to bed.

He got a beer from the fridge and finished it standing there and then took another and sat down at the table and sifted through the ashtrays looking for a passable cigarette butt. His mind tried to picture how it had been – half the glory is in the remembering – but nothing would emerge from the night's dark shadows.

Too bad, he thought. A loss and a shame. Life has so few precious moments. Only a drunken fool would fail to bank them.

He sighed and gave up his search and sat staring morosely at the whiskey bottle tucked under the sink. It had been presented full and but a third remained and his hostess never exceeded her limit. So he'd put half of it away, and a few beers for chasers, and carrying a load upon arrival, too? He told himself it was a handy thing that one didn't get spat upon daily.

Bogna came into the kitchen and caught him at it. 'Not already,' she said. 'I was hoping you'd spare me the remorse.'

Shaver looked up wondering why she would want to start that. 'I mourn for thee,' he told her, flicking at an ashtray. 'Your genteel poverty. One can tell a lot about a place from its cigarette butts – and here they're smoked the shortest in town.'

'You're out?'

'Yes.'

There was a moment's hesitation and then she crossed to the sideboard and pulled open a drawer and dug around at the back. A package was produced and she tossed it at him sullenly. Sweet Caps. Stale.

'A woman's intuition,' she said. 'I knew you'd be around sooner or later. So naturally I saw to the provisions.'

Shaver got one out and lit it and was hard put not to make a face. The tobacco was as dry as a leaf found pressed in some old book. Had he really been that long between visits?

'You're welcome,' Bogna said. She slammed the drawer and tightened her robe – a bad sign, that – and busied herself at the sink, more intent on making noise than coffee. 'What did it this time?'

'Did what?' Shaver asked. He would never understand women. Five minutes ago she had been singing.

'Don't be quaint,' she said. 'The last time, as I recall, it was the Middle East oil crisis, and the time before, the Sino-Soviet border clashes . . .' She stopped, unhappy with her sarcasm, as well she might be, for it was not up to her usual high standards. 'Forget I asked.'

'You don't care?'

'No.'

Liar, Shaver thought. He drank his beer and sat staring at her stiff back. She had never been a beauty, but her age permitted her that pretense now, and there was also something about her – perhaps the agony that was so quick to show in her eyes? – that held a certain attraction for him. Nor, he reminded himself, was she without other attributes, such as a good education, and a solid set of values, and an appreciation for the finer things, and even manners when she chose to use them. Not at all bad for a Polack. But the main thing was that she was so goddam thankful.

'Why should I?' Bogna asked, banging dishes. 'Do you care about me? Have you ever cared about me?'

'That's a nice question,' Shaver said, glad she had her back turned. One day, he thought, his face was going to betray him, and then she wouldn't ask that anymore, because she'd finally have her answer.

'Hah,' Bogna said.

Shaver didn't answer. The one sure way to avoid an argument. He sat drinking his beer and wishing that he hadn't got quite so tanked up before arriving on her doorstep. If he'd had his wits about him, he could have asked his favor then, and the thing would be settled and his purpose accomplished. Bogna would promise him anything before the

33

fact. It was only after the ecstasy that she raged for a permanent place in paradise.

He sat quietly for a long while, letting her take it out on the dishes, patiently waiting for the right moment. After yesterday, he couldn't afford any more mistakes, he thought. He could still feel Henke's hot foul breath on his face. The smell of sickbed linen – and then the yellow sticky spittle hitting him.

Henke watched the bath water run out of his tub, the small congealed wads of his sperm disappearing with it, the very gift of life being swept down a dark hole by the relentless forces at work deep in the bowels of the earth. He felt a terrible burning shame. He had sinned again.

If only, Henke thought, his flat eyes moving to the page torn from *Playboy*. There were three naked girls, one putting on lipstick, another brushing her leg with poster paint, and a third just standing there, her head back, her long hair dangling, her eyes closed, and her lips parted.

It struck him that he ought to read the caption. 'Alice Ottawa (below left) enjoys dancing in the Düsseldorf Company and heartily supports the anti-political, anti-war themes of the show. New York's Salley Eaton (bottom left), like many cast members, makes astral projections for her own future (her sign is Aries with Aquarius rising). Gayle Hayden (below right), of the San Francisco company, is a Libra born in neighboring Palo Alto.'

Anti-political? Anti-war? Henke told himself that was just like a woman. They might be beautiful on the outside but what about the inside? There was no telling what they were really like until it was too late. Until they had you trapped.

It's a hell of a life without a wife, Henke thought, the old ditty coming to mind unbidden. *And a damned sight worse with one.*

That made him feel better. Any saying ridiculing the marital status served to cheer him. He had dozens stored away for instant replay whenever the opportunity presented itself. *Another war declared*, voiced at the sight of a newly married couple driving away from the ceremony, was his all-time favorite. That said it all.

He thought of this and a number of other apt declarations on the wisdom of being a bachelor and soon his guilt was assuaged. He wasn't the only man who had chosen not to marry, he reminded himself. There were hundreds of thousands who had made the same choice. Probably millions.

That large a number, he argued, proved there was nothing wrong with him, because if there was something wrong with him, that meant there was something wrong with all the others, too. You couldn't just single him out from millions of men and say there was something wrong with him and not the others.

It wasn't as if he was some sort of weirdo, Henke thought. God knows he had the right urges. He thought of women, not horses, when he was doing it, didn't he? It was women he dreamed of at night. It was women he thought of doing all those things ...

Enough, Henke decided. There was no need to justify himself. He was perfectly *normal* and he was unmarried by *choice*, and just because he had *certain standards*, just because he didn't go chasing, lusting and whoring, begging and buying ...

What was that?

Henke listened for a moment. The knock came again.

Oh, God, Henke thought. Not the soul-savers. There was a new bunch every goddam Sunday. He'd really tell them off this time.

Henke screwed the top back on his shampoo lubricant and eased his bulk out of the tub. 'It's a Prell of a life,' he whispered, grinning in anticipation.

Finally Bogna broke the silence. 'The coffee's ready,' she said, still facing the sink. 'Would you mind pouring me a cup? Or is that beyond the realm of your services?'

'I could make an exception, I guess,' Shaver said easily. He got up and took the pot off the gas and filled the two cups she had set out on the sideboard. 'Seeing as how it's you.'

'Thanks, bastard,' she told him.

He grinned at her and took his own cup back to the table and sat down again. He watched as she dried her hands and examined her face in the little mirror over the sink and adjusted the combs holding up her long straw-colored hair.

'I'm in trouble,' he said then. The words came out flat and defiant, like he was simply stating a fact, not asking for help of any kind, and even suggesting that it would be refused if offered.

Bogna stared at him over the rim of her coffee cup. Obviously, she wanted to say, but her anger had subsided now, washed away with the grease from the dishes, and she sensed that this was a different problem from the ones he usually brought her. 'Bad?' she asked.

He nodded. 'Yes.'

'Well,' Bogna said. She leaned against the sink and sipped at her coffee. 'Do you want to tell me about it?'

'I can't,' Shaver said. 'It's got something to do with a new assignment they've given me.' He looked up at her. 'You hadn't heard I got switched to Special Branch?'

'Special Branch?' Bogna said. It was obvious that she was surprised. 'That's something I missed . . .' Her expression changed to one of puzzlement. 'How could they do that before your hearing?'

'Easy,' Shaver said. 'They just do it.' He sipped carefully at the scalding hot coffee. 'You should know that by now. If it suits their purpose, they'll throw away the rule book, and pity the dumb bastard who yells foul.'

'You're really working again?'

'Unofficially.'

'Well,' Bogna said. 'Good for you. Plus a transfer to Special Branch . . .' She stopped and the puzzled expression was back. 'So what's the problem? That's hardly call for getting falling-down drunk.'

'You think not?' Shaver asked. 'I've nearly buggered my debut, that's all. They gave me a hot potato and I dropped it right off.' He blew on the coffee and took another sip. 'My own fault, too. Putting on a show.'

Bogna hesitated while she considered the propriety of her next question. Until now, they had followed an unwritten rule. If classified information was involved, they left the job at the office. The rule wasn't that essential – after all, she held the more sensitive position, didn't she? – but it was still a good idea. Careless talk could lead to needless trouble.

'It's nothing that hush-hush,' Shaver said, ending her dilemma. 'There's a man they want taken out of circulation for a few days, that's all. An enforced vacation at the expense of the crown. A piece of cake, I thought, but he spotted me following him, and now he's on his guard. He's also a lot smarter than I had imagined. Smarter and perhaps tougher.'

'You make it sound important.'

'It is.' Shaver took another drink of coffee and then pushed the cup away. 'I've got the awful feeling that the outcome of my hearing hinges on me doing a good job. They practically came out and said so.'

'They wouldn't do that,' Bogna said firmly.

'You think not?' Shaver said. 'You're the girl who keeps the records. How many non-coms can you recall who've got away with bopping an officer?'

'There's been some,' she told him. 'And besides you're something special, aren't you? They're not going to let you go that easily ...' She moved over to the table and stood smiling down at him. 'I also have it on good authority that you acted under extreme provocation.'

'That there was,' Shaver laughed. 'I'm pleading self-defense. I was only protecting my sweet young body from forcible rape. Everybody warned me that he was trying to screw me.'

'So why worry?'

'I wasn't worried before,' Shaver admitted. 'But I am now with this new case fouled up. It's the kind of dicey situation that could go either way.' He laughed to demonstrate his bravery in the teeth of such implacable odds. 'It's funny how I blew it. Tell me the truth now. Ten good reasons why I shouldn't pass for a newspaper writer.'

'You?' Bogna said. She felt the relief sweep over her. He'd only been trying to frighten her. The bastard wasn't at the gallows quite yet. 'Your face, for one thing, I suppose. It's no good for a newspaper type. Some small inkling of intelligence is required.' A pause to think what further harm she could do him. 'But you might be accepted as one of their lower life forms. Perhaps a legman.'

'Me?' Shaver said. 'Don't be silly. You know me better than that. I've always been a tit man.' He grabbed for the hem of her robe. 'Come here.'

That was the wrong thing for him to do. It reminded her that she was hard done by and that she was supposed to be angry. 'Keep your paws to yourself,' she complained, kicking at him. 'Who the hell do you think you are?'

'I didn't think an introduction was necessary.'

'That's what makes me mad,' she said, 'your goddam supreme self-confidence. Did it ever occur to you that I might say no? Is it so far-fetched to imagine that I might have other callers?'

'I telephoned first,' he said mildly.

'Jesus Christ,' Bogna breathed. 'That's not the point ...' The hurt was suddenly shimmering on her face. 'Can't you understand? That's *not* the point.'

Well, Shaver thought, we're off again, and it's a pity your head isn't clearer, chum. Mary Martyr is her finest role. She suffers so beautifully.

'I know,' he said. 'I only come when I need solace, and there are times when you need it, too.' He turned away so he wouldn't have to look at her. 'The point is that I'm never here then. I only come to take – not to give.'

She made a sound that was part tears and part laughter. 'Then why don't you do something about it?'

'You mean come around more often?'

'Why not? Would that be so difficult?'

'Not initially,' Shaver said, careful in his answer. 'It might even prove quite pleasant ...' He saw that he still had some beer left in the bottle sitting on the table. He picked it up and pretended to examine the label. 'But sooner or later it would become a chore.'

'*Chore?*'

'Chore,' Shaver repeated. 'Variously defined as a routine job or a hard task. You can look it up if you want confirmation.' He finished off the beer and handed her the empty bottle. 'Mind telling me where you put my trousers?'

Bogna looked at the bottle inanely and for a moment it seemed she might put it with the other empties. Then, finally, her higher instincts prevailed, and it shattered on the wall dangerously close to Shaver's head.

'Missed,' Shaver noted. He picked his way through the broken glass and went into the bathroom and slammed the door and locked it and then hung over the sink trying to find a shred of sense in what had happened. He seriously wondered if what she had might be catching. Could her propensity for self-destruction be contagious?

The face in the mirror stared back at him mockingly. There were never any answers there. Tired gray eyes, and a nose that hadn't mended properly, and a mouth that didn't laugh enough, and a permanently dazed expression, slight but nevertheless noticeable, particularly if you were told to look for it.

'You poor dumb bugger,' Shaver said.

He found a razor in the medicine cabinet and scraped off the night's collection of stubble and then blundered into the tub and turned the taps on full. All the better to drown the anguish, he thought, and he stood there, stupefied, until the water ran so cold that he couldn't bear it any longer.

Mother Mac knocked for the fifth time on the door of her top-floor tenant. The only reason she persisted was that she had walked up two flights of stairs with her message and that was a considerable effort for a woman of her girth. She did not want to see the trip wasted.

'You drunken sot,' she finally cried. 'You damn well better open this door. I know you're in there.'

There was no answer and she placed her ear against a panel and listened for any indication that life might persist beyond the thin barrier.

'Come on,' she roared, thoroughly exasperated. 'You better get your lazy ass out of the fart sack. I'm kicking my way in otherwise.'

'My dear lady,' a voice answered. 'My dear, sweet, gentle lady. Let me assure you . . .' There was the sound of hurried movements and at last the door opened. 'Let me assure you that I find your vulgar mouth most offensive and that I am particularly shattered by your threats of violence on this, the Lord's Day. It is very definitely *not* couth.'

'You sure took your time,' Mother Mac said.

'I was putting on my robe,' Petapiece told her, eyes puffed with sleep. 'Despite my present misfortune, I come from quite good stock, actually.' He grimaced as his tongue began to advise him of the taste in his mouth. 'A gentleman, I was.'

'Huh,' Mother Mac said. Her disdainful gaze moved down his robe. 'I don't know what you've got to hide. A skinny runt like you.'

'You'd be surprised.'

'Would I now?'

'Come, come,' Petapiece said. 'You're not propositioning me again, are you? You have my answer. Lips that touch wine . . .'

'Jesus in his glory,' Mother Mac said, shaking her head. 'Why do I get all the nuts? A dozen flophouses in the block and they all come stay with me.' She stood aside so he'd have room to pass. 'There's a telephone call for you.'

'Me?' Petapiece said in genuine surprise. He had no important cases running. Nothing that would necessitate someone contacting him here. Unless . . .

'You,' he was assured.

'Well,' Petapiece said. 'Why don't I answer it then? Probably my broker.' He slipped past and hurried down the stairs. 'He's been pestering me about soybean features.'

'Sure,' Mother Mac said. She sighed heavily and started down after him.

Petapiece was almost finished saying. 'It's as good as done. It's probably happening right now.'

Mother Mac stopped and made no pretense about her eavesdropping. She'd earned the right with that climb.

'Listen,' Petapiece said, obviously angry. 'Have I ever failed you? Have I ever messed up even once?' He stood listening impatiently and then broke into his caller's conversation. 'All right, for Christ's sake. *All right*. I let you know just as soon as it happens. The precise instant.'

Mother Mac stood staring at him unsurely as he hung up. 'Something wrong?'

'No,' Petapiece said. He winked at her and started back up the stairs. How could anything possibly go wrong? Success depended on Corporal Shaver – and the corporal was an idiot.

When Shaver came out of the bathroom, Bogna was lying face down on the bed, her face buried in a pillow, her fists clenched tightly, and one leg kicked back at the knee. The classic position, Shaver thought. He wondered why it wasn't listed in any of the how-to-do-it books. Few things did more to rub a man's loins.

'You're so filthy to me,' Bogna sobbed. 'You treat me like some cheap whore . . .' Her robe rippled with the wretched cries tearing from deep inside her body. 'Get out, God damn you! Get out!'

Shaver grabbed her roughly by the shoulders and rolled her over and dropped heavily on top of her.

'No!' she screamed, fighting him, stronger than she should be, but his weight held her pinned. She struggled that way, first cursing, then crying, and then in a quiet desperation, the only sounds her heavy breathing and her heart hammering like some machine run amok.

'I'll leave if you want,' Shaver told her. He ripped open her robe and her breasts fell out, huge melons in his hands, overripe, dangling. 'I'll go and never come back. Who needs you?'

Bogna ceased to struggle. Her body went limp, a soft, pliant, rubbery pillow. She lay lost in surrender while he nursed her passion and then at last her hands went down to grasp and lead him into her suddenly plunging thighs. 'You do,' she cried fiercely.

She was right, Shaver thought, smiling. He could use her help, and it was his intention to ask soon, but meanwhile she was welcome to stick it in. Shaver told himself that he wasn't the kind to quarrel with one more sweaty tumble. Where was the harm in an act of love?

Four

At ten o'clock Monday morning Shaver drove a plain black late-model Plymouth into the public parking lot across from the Lost Lagoon tennis courts in Stanley Park. The lot was empty and probably would remain that way throughout the day. It was too wet and cold for tennis and the nearby pitch-and-putt course was closed Mondays.

Shaver parked at the extreme northeast corner, a position where, through a narrow buffer strip of maple trees, he had a fairly clear view of Henke's rooming house at the foot of Barclay Street. He couldn't see the front door – a thick ever-green in the yard obscured that – but the porch stairs were visible, as well as the sidewalk leading to the street. Henke would have to leave by the rear for Shaver to miss him, and that wasn't worth worrying about. There was one good thing you could say for Henke. He was predictable.

Shaver had it all planned. It was going to be daring, but it was also going to be very simple and straightforward. As Henke started walking down the hill to the bus stop, Shaver was going to ride the Plymouth upon the sidewalk, blocking Henke's path, and he was going to leap out of the car with his gun drawn. 'Police – hold it right there,' Shaver was going to say, and he was going to have Henke handcuffed and in the car in about ten seconds flat, and any witnesses to this little drama were going to be still standing bug-eyed when he drove away.

It would work, Shaver told himself. The element of the completely unexpected – the car suddenly jumping up on the sidewalk – would make it work. There wasn't a person in a thousand who wouldn't be badly rattled when that hap-pened to him and Henke certainly didn't look like the exception. He would be too shaken to put up a fight or even to try making a run for it. He'd still be in shock when the gun was pushed into his gut and the handcuffs snapped on his wrists.

The more Shaver thought about the plan, the better he liked it, and the irony was that Henke, in a sense, had written the script. If Henke hadn't screamed pig – if the lop-eared bastard had simply ignored the friendly overtures and walked away – he'd still be wrestling with a bunch of imaginary problems, Shaver thought. It had been a big mistake to start out playing kidnaper and trying to think as a criminal planning a crime. The criminal viewpoint presented all sorts of hurdles. But when he was finally forced to look at the assignment from the proper perspective – as a police officer, not a criminal, and with the idea that he was taking someone into custody, not actually kidnaping them – the myriad of difficulties he had conjured up simply melted away.

It would be easy, Shaver thought. So very, very easy. The whole thing was the timing. If he could just get the timing right ...

Like, now, he told himself, starting the Plymouth. He backed up carefully, eased out of the lot, turned north on Lagoon Drive, and then picked up speed as he cut onto Chilco and headed down the hill toward the trolley-bus turn-around at Georgia Street.

Now, he repeated, hurtling past the opening to the lane north of Haro. He raised his left hand from the wheel to look at his watch. Forty-eight seconds.

Shaver drove back to the lot and parked in the same space. He slouched down in his seat and opened a fresh pouch of Sweet Caps. He sat smoking and watching the front of Henke's rooming house.

To hell with Bogna, Shaver thought. If she couldn't do him a small favor, that was her tough luck, not his. He didn't need her help. He could handle this by himself.

Bogna stared unhappily at the teletype message from the computer at the Central Data File at RCMP Headquarters in Ottawa. RE VCR RQST RUDOLPH HENKE FILE SUMMARY. SBJCT FILE CLASSIFIED TOP SECRET, ADVS RECIPIENT AND AUTHOR-IZATION.

That just proved it, Bogna thought. She should have stuck to her decision and not sent the request. It was bad enough to ask for any sort of confidential material without proper authorization. But top secret?

Damn him, she cursed. Damn him, damn him, damn him. Shaver shouldn't have asked her to do it. It was his own fault he'd been suspended and what was he doing working on an undercover job before his hearing? It was so dumb to get himself into that kind of a fix – and it was especially stupid that he had to be devious about seeing a file connected with the case.

Bogna tore the message off the machine – her intent was to destroy it – and then quickly changed her mind. She would have to send some sort of answer, she thought. Otherwise the miserable computer would keep pestering.

She sat down prepared to send a cancellation and then changed her mind again. There was no turning back at this stage, she decided. Someone checking the teletype file copy might think it strange that a request for material was canceled simply because it was classified. She quickly typed her answer. RUDOLPH HENKE FILE SUMMARY RECIPIENT MCDERMOTT CIB VCR AUTHORIZATION M2502B.

Well, Bogna thought, staring at it. You've really put your neck in the noose now, haven't you, lady? Contravention of the Official Secrets Act.

A small shiver ran through her and she wondered if Shaver would be properly appreciative.

Shaver looked at his watch and felt the first little stabs of doubt start to do their evil work. It was half-past twelve, and still no sign of Henke, and where the hell was he?

He's *got* to come out, because that's his pattern, damn it, Shaver kept thinking, but he knew he was only kidding himself. No pattern ever held forever – the only true constant was change – and there could be a million reasons why Henke had veered from the norm today.

Shaver started with the explanation he found most palatable. Henke had simply slept in. He'd be out soon enough and everything would proceed as planned. But it was equally possible, of course, that Henke wasn't feeling well and had decided to stay home for the day. It was also possible that he had left the house before ten o'clock. Or had gone at the usual time but had sneaked out the back door. Or . . .

No, Shaver thought, trying to close his mind to what, in truth, was the most logical explanation. Alerted by their confrontation on the bus, Henke had moved out of the flat and gone into hiding, where the lop-eared bastard would remain perfectly safe – until.

Until what? Shaver wondered if the KGB was correct in its assessment and that Henke might actually make some move against Kosygin. If Henke did plan something . . . and if the business on the bus had sent him into hiding . . . and if he couldn't be located before Kosygin's arrival . . .

'Bury me now,' Shaver muttered. He looked at his watch and decided he should wait a while longer. It would be stupid to panic, he thought. Only idiots panicked.

Bogna had a girl friend pick her up a sandwich rather than go out for lunch. She wanted to be standing over the teletype machine when Henke's file summary came in from Ottawa. If one of the communications clerks got it first, it would be stuffed into a pneumatic tube and sent directly to the CIB, and there would be some embarrassing questions asked when it ended up on Inspector McDermott's desk.

Never again, Bogna promised herself, a mouthful of the sandwich going down with difficulty. This was the first and last time she'd ever bend the rules for anybody. Her stomach had been doing cartwheels ever since she had sent McDermott's clearance number to Central Data. For the tenth time, she thought that she should have used Shaver's number, and then immediately reversed herself once more, using the equally persistent argument that the all-knowing computer probably was aware of Shaver's suspension.

Bogna threw away the rest of the sandwich and stood staring miserably at the stuttering keys holding at the left margin. The teletype had just completed taking descriptions of new additions to the fugitives' list, and stolen cars would be next, no doubt. Anything to keep up the suspense and torture.

Never, Bogna promised. Never, ever, again, and then the machine started and she breathed a heavy sigh of relief. Here it was at last. ATTN MCDERMOTT CIB VCR, TOP SECRET RPT TOP SECRET. RUDOLPH HENKE FILE SUMMARY FOLLOWS...

Bogna cleared the previous messages, so that she could tear off the summary as soon as it was completed, and when she looked back, only a few seconds later, she was surprised to find the computer signing off. The summary comprised just one paragraph.

That's hardly possible, Bogna thought, and then she read it and discovered why it was so brief, and suddenly she found herself laughing. No wonder Shaver had been told there was nothing of importance in Henke's file. Considering the assignment they'd given him, he'd be beside himself if he saw this, wouldn't he? Absolutely beside himself.

Bogna thought it was such a joke that she couldn't stop laughing.

Shaver put his hands in his raincoat pocket and fingered his pouch of Sweet Caps. There were only two cigarettes left and it was barely past six o'clock. He'd get cancer for sure, he thought. If he didn't die of pneumonia first. It was raining slightly, hardly more than a drizzle, but he'd been out in it for almost four hours, prowling back and forth like a frustrated animal, and the damp cold had gotten into his bones.

Shaver felt sure that Henke wasn't in his flat. If he had stayed home, there ought to be a light showing somewhere by now, even if the man was ill, but there wasn't the faintest glimmer at any of the attic windows. The possibility that Henke had gone into hiding also loomed greater with each passing minute. Normally, he was home before six, a bag of groceries on his arm, and so another part of the routine had been shattered.

Yet Shaver remained reluctant to go up and check. Despite all the evidence to the contrary, Henke could be home, purposely holed up or perhaps just sleeping the day through, and Shaver didn't want a confrontation before he was prepared to take the man into custody. Another incident like the one on the bus would really put him on his guard.

If he went into the house at all, he should push through with his grab-and-run plan, Shaver thought. There was the chance it might work there just as well as on the street. The police were no strangers at Henke's door, after all. He'd been arrested several times in the past year. His fellow tenants would consider it normal enough to see him being taken away again.

But surely this was a last resort best suited for a late-night foray? If he could possibly avoid it, Shaver didn't want any witnesses, and God forbid, he certainly didn't want any interference from them. You could never tell who might get involved if your prisoner started screaming – especially if you didn't have a warrant.

The pro and con arguments kept banging around inside Shaver's skull. Go up. Hold back. Act now. Wait . . .

Go up and check, damn you, Shaver thought, fingering the flattened cigarette pouch. It's hundred to one he's not there and you've got no more excuses for delaying any longer. If he'd come home for supper it would solve your dilemma, but he hasn't and now you've got to go up and check. If Henke has run off, you should be sounding the alarm, not standing here in the rain like a fool.

Shaver smoked his last cigarettes one after another – a condemned man's right, he thought, unsmiling – and then crossed the street and strode purposefully toward the rooming house. He felt better with his first step. It was the not knowing that ate away at him.

The new mood didn't last long. His spirits sagged again as soon as he pushed open the front door and saw the ten mail boxes bunched together in the vestibule. The day's small traffic in and out had provided no warning that so many lived here and he wondered where and how they all fitted. Ackerman, Perdowski, Goldfarb, Fitzpatrick, Mendelssohn . . .

Ten tenants, by God, he thought reaching the end at last, and the house originally built for one family, and how could he possibly run such a gauntlet?

No answer came to mind. Just the thought that if Henke was home it would be a lot easier for everyone concerned if he simply killed the lop-eared bastard. Why not? he mused. Take this Henke chap out of circulation, Petapiece had

47

instructed, and he obviously was concerned with results, not finesse. Special Branch had given its word on the matter and it wouldn't do at all not to come through. A promise is a promise, and when it's made to the Russians, especially so.

Shaver laughed softly and started up the stairs. So it was murder, bloody murder, that he was contemplating now, was it? What a side-splitter.

Still, he thought, a step squeaking underfoot, there were no ironclad guarantees that blood wouldn't be spilled. So many things could go wrong and you couldn't just stand there if your man drew a gun or started punching. He'd have to be subdued then, and you never knew, exactly and for sure, how much force might be required. The softest-looking Buster Boy could turn tiger when cornered . . .

Shaver stopped abruptly at the first landing. Up ahead, a door had opened a crack, and Shaver could physically feel the staring eyes upon him. Oh, grand, he thought. Wasn't this just what he needed? Some scummy spy to describe him to a *t*? He considered turning back and trying again later but immediately rejected the idea. He had wasted far too much time already. This had to be done now.

Shaver gathered up his strength and went boldly down the hall and heard the door open behind him. 'What number did you want?'

'Ten,' Shaver said, turning to face his inquisitor. Perhaps then the man wouldn't scream so loudly.

'Henke, eh?' a gnomelike creature said. 'He's upstairs. The only one there. Got the whole attic.' He opened his door wider and the light showed a cruelly humped back and a thin bent leg in a brace. 'Bill collector?'

Shaver shook his head and walked back a few steps. This crooked little stick would have the whole damn house alerted soon. There'd be a dozen more crowding around him, desperate for news of the outside world, pummeling him with their merciless questions.

'Police then?'

'Yes,' Shaver admitted, showing his badge. His course had been set by those two questions. To say a friend would have aroused suspicions. 'I was hoping to make it a surprise.'

'Ah,' the cripple said. 'Another warrant, eh? That's the

third this year.' He squeezed his good leg against the door jamb in a vain attempt to contain a large yellow cat. 'Grab him, will you?'

Shaver reached down without thinking and then pulled away too late. The back of his hand had three long red slashes on it.

'You startled him,' the cripple complained. He hobbled off in pursuit, his leg brace thumping with every step, and the cat, having long experience at this chase, kept just far enough ahead.

Shaver stood stricken as they turned up the stairs. He was committed to the thing now. If Henke was home, he'd have to grab him, but he didn't want the whole house watching, damn it. He prayed for a miracle and had the worst realized when the cat was cornered at the top.

'Got you!' the cripple cried, pouncing, and the animal let out a howl that could be heard on the street below.

Shaver finally got his feet to move. If the door opened, he had to be there, ready to thrust himself inside. Give Henke the chance to slam it shut and all was lost. He'd be on the phone to his lousy liberal lawyers while the lock was still being kicked off.

'You're a real rascal, you are, Wilbur,' the yellow terror was advised, embraced as a wayward son. 'What do you think you'll find up here? Some stray pussy?' A bone-grinding squeeze snuffed out any hope of reply. 'He's a bad one. Always running away. I don't know what to do with him.'

'Have you ever considered That Big Kitty Litter in the Sky?' Shaver said, his hand smarting worse than ever. He positioned himself before the door and stood in sweating anticipation. With his luck there'd be a night chain. Precise timing was crucial.

The cripple edged in for a closer view, discernibly licking his lips, and soon became impatient at Shaver's technique. 'It might help if you knocked,' he said.

'What for?' Shaver muttered. 'Have you no faith in Wilbur? He could rouse the dead.'

A door opened somewhere below them – a coffin lid creaking in support of this contention – and a disembodied voice floated in the stairwell. 'Is everything all right up there?'

'Tell her yes,' Shaver instructed, lying through his teeth. He took a deep breath and rapped sharply. This was rapidly getting out of hand. He hadn't counted on half so many witnesses.

'Perhaps he's not home,' the cripple said. 'I haven't seen him for a while. Not since Sunday.'

Nor I, Shaver thought, knocking again. He wondered how he could have been so desperate as to be driven to this intolerable situation. Desperation was a lousy chauffeur. 'That wouldn't be the landlady?'

'No. That's Number Four. Mrs. Goldfarb.'

'Is she coming up?'

'Try stopping her.'

Shaver knocked once more, good measure, and then threw the thing in, resigned to another botch. It was plain that Henke was not at home, and even if he was, he was past admitting it.

'You're going to break in?'

'No.'

'Oh,' the cripple said sadly, failing to hide his disappointment. He looked at the door a long moment – seeing it in splinters would make his winter – and then hastened to salvage what he could. 'What's the charge this time?'

'Two dollars,' Shaver told him. 'You'll never get a better bargain. I haven't put on a show like this for years.'

Five

Bogna made sure that her door was locked. All the way home, she had felt like a fugitive criminal, expecting any moment that a heavy hand would be laid on her arm, and she wouldn't feel safe until Henke's file summary was out of her purse and safely hidden.

The secret life of Rudolph Henke might be a big joke on Shaver, but it would be no laughing matter if she was caught outside the office with classified material in her possession, Bogna thought, hastily removing her hat and coat.

She'd lose more than her job for that. She'd end up in court and there'd be a fine and possibly a jail sentence. And all for what? The look on Shaver's face?

Yes, she admitted. That's why she had made a copy of the teletype message and brought it home. To see that look.

She swore at herself for being so stupid – just as stupid as Shaver – and anxiously surveyed the living room for a good place. If she could just get the damn thing properly hidden, she could finally rest in peace. She was out of the woods at the office. The original message, supposedly initialed by McDermott, had already gone through the shredder, blocking that avenue of discovery. The carbon copy of the day's teletype run had been sent to storage and that was almost as good as having it destroyed. The chance of McDermott's personally checking the carbons was nil – and who but McDermott would wonder what the hell when he saw a summary he actually hadn't requested or received?

Bogna's eye was caught by a favored object on the fireplace mantel. That was such an obvious hiding place. And yet ...?

Part of the joke, Bogna thought, laughing

Shaver left the car and walked to English Bay, punishing

himself in the damp cold, and creating still more of an excuse, however transparent, for a warming supply of rum at the Sylvia. The truth was that he sorely needed some Dutch courage. He'd be going back to the rooming house when the last light was out, and he'd be getting confirmation that Henke had indeed run off somewhere, and then he'd be faced with the prospect of telling Petapiece.

That part, he thought, shivering, could wait until morning. By the time he searched Henke's flat The Stump Club would be closed and he knew no other way to contact Petapiece. Shaver argued with himself that this didn't matter and that morning was soon enough. There was no sense sounding an alert in the middle of the night. No real search would start until the morning, regardless.

Sure, Shaver grimaced, wondering who he was fooling. The thought of Petapiece – he could picture him sitting and waiting and wondering – began to prey on his mind. He had promised Monday and the day was almost gone and it would be shitty to let the deadline pass without a word one way or the other.

By the time he reached the hotel, Shaver was seriously considering a telephone call to The Stump Club, and when he entered the lobby and saw that the pay phone was free, it was like an omen.

Petapiece had given him a rule – no unnecessary contacts – and that, when translated, meant he'd prefer not to hear from him until the job was done, but Shaver's stomach argued otherwise. Shaver had a very queasy feeling about what the day had brought and what the night might hold. He felt on the verge of throwing up.

That gut feeling people were always talking about, no doubt, Shaver thought. He looked up the number and placed his call and wondered how much he dare say over the telephone. He wished that he'd had more experience with Special Branch. This was one of those moments where a certain style and finesse were required and he could only think of one awful line. It seems our pigeon has flown the coop.

The phone rang half a dozen times before being answered by a tired voice. Shaver was disappointed that he didn't recognize it. He had hoped to get the bartender he had met earlier. They'd got on rather well when Shaver had made out the application for his club membership and a friendly voice would help now.

'Who?' the new man said. 'Black John? I don't think so . . .' The phone clattered on the bar – from the background noise, it was a livelier place come evening, Shaver thought – and there was a long wait before it was picked up again. 'No. He's not around. Hasn't been all day.'

'You're sure?' Shaver asked.

'Yes,' he was told. 'It's a double shift for me. Bertie's down with the flu.'

'You must be tired.'

'I'm dead. You can order the casket.'

Shaver mumbled something appropriate and rang off wondering what sin of his had prompted this whirlwind. He told himself that mere coincidence couldn't explain two disappearances in one day. That mean a blow required divine guidance.

He started for the Sylvia's bar – he was thinking that he'd have more than just one drink – but the newspaper on display in a nearby coin box stopped him. KOSYGIN VISIT FIRM, the headline said. DUE WEDNESDAY NIGHT IN VANCOUVER.

Only two more days, Shaver thought. Two fleeting days. A small surge of panic hit him – felt himself standing helpless in the face of some irreversible process – and for some reason he thought of Bogna. Right now he'd give an arm to know what others knew of Henke. Was it possible that she had changed her mind?

Shaver returned to the pay phone and placed the call and Bogna answered on the first ring and sounded unusually happy.

'So soon?' she said. 'I must be living right. Where are you?'

'The West End.'

'Coming around?'

'No.'

'Too bad,' Bogna said, laughing. 'You know that F-I-L-E you wanted? I managed it this afternoon.'

'That's why I called,' Shaver said, barely able to speak. 'There's something come up. I could use a little help from my friends.'

'Over the phone? You're aware of what you're suggesting, are you, X-5? A possible compromise.'

'Don't fiddle with me. This could be important.'

'What would M-15 think?'

'*Please.*'

'Or is it MI-5? They're all so confusing. What's a poor girl to do?'

'Listen, damn it!' Shaver shouted. 'Don't you hear me? I said that file could be important.'

'Then come and get it,' Bogna said, still laughing, and she hung up.

Shaver slammed down the phone. The bitch, he thought. She probably didn't have it. That was just an excuse to get him over. If she had the file and there was something important in it, she wouldn't be making a joke of the thing, would she?

The desk clerk eyed him critically from across the lobby. 'May I help you, sir?' the clerk said.

'No,' Shaver said, and then, not wanting to be curt, provided an explanation. 'I am beyond assistance.' He turned up his collar and plunged out into the night.

Petapiece sidled up to the bar at The Stump Club.

'Busy isn't it?' he said, taking the bottle of ale that was passed without his asking. 'Strange for a Monday. I've never seen it like this before.'

The bartender nodded in agreement. 'God punishing me. He heard about my double shift.'

'You've been working all day?' Petapiece said. 'No wonder you're looking peaked. There ought to be a law.'

'A union, you mean,' the bartender said. He pushed his cash drawer shut and retrieved his wet rag and mopped at the bar dispiritedly.

Petapiece offered no comment either way. The subject held too much potential for argument, and, within reason, he wanted to keep on the good side of the help. The Stump Club was one of the best meeting places he had run across in a long time and he planned to use it for a while. Where else could he have a reserved table – well, practically reserved, anyway – for a lousy fifteen dollars a year? The small correction was necessary because his table happened to be taken tonight due to the unusually large crowd. Normally, the place was half empty, even on a Saturday, and the other members were careful to steer away from the corner they called Black John's.

'Say,' the bartender said. 'I almost forgot. You had two telephone calls.'

'Two, huh?' Petapiece said. He climbed up on one of the bar stools and took a long pull on his ale. 'Both from the same guy?'

The bartender shrugged. 'I dunno. No names as usual. But they was sounding kinda worried.'

'You don't say?' Petapiece laughed and took another drink and examined the crowd in the mirror behind the bar. The place was really swinging tonight.

'Real worried,' the bartender said, tossing down his rag. 'Desperate even.' He stood staring for a moment at Petapiece. 'Where in the hell have you been all day anyway?'

'Avoiding telephone calls,' Petapiece said, laughing again. He wondered why the Yul Brynner character was looking so goddam pleased with himself. The cat that swallowed the canary – and you could practically see the feathers around his mouth.

Wilbur and his friend were waiting patiently on the second-floor landing. The Barclay Street Death Watch – not to be denied their carrion. 'You're back?' the taller of the two asked needlessly.

'Yes,' Shaver admitted, caught out as it were. 'You're in for a rare treat. The Midnight Skulker strikes again.' He stopped to catch his breath and glanced up significantly at Number Ten. 'Any sign of life?'

'No. Nothing since you left. I've been watching the whole time.'

I'll bet, Shaver thought. Name any wager. My balls if you want and you're covered. 'Strange . . .'

'Isn't it?' was the eager reply. 'Not like him at all. He's

usually staggering around drunk this time of night.' There was a pause to savor the next part. 'Do you think something's gone wrong?'

'Such as?' Shaver asked, looking away. It was revolting to witness such anticipation.

'He could be dead up there.'

'That's possible, I suppose,' Shaver said. 'Or sick. Or lying in wait to spring a trap . . .' He unbuttoned his raincoat and reached inside. 'Certainly it warrants looking.'

'A trap?'

'I'll need a lookout,' Shaver said. 'If you could stay in your room, the door open a crack, watching the stairs for me.' He made a grand production of unholstering his Webley. 'Is there something you could use to signal?'

The cripple looked at the gun and there was one less volunteer for the sortie. 'What's that for?'

'What do you think?' Shaver asked grimly, marveling at how easy he could think up lies. 'I'm just back from the hospital and the man he hit is dead. It's no longer a case of simple assault. It's the small matter of murder.'

'Murder?'

'Shush,' Shaver said. 'You want the hall full of people, do you? You want that responsibility when the lead starts flying?'

'You think it might come to that?'

Shaver checked the Webley's chamber and was careless where the barrel pointed. 'The psychiatrist says he's probably a psycho. Did he ever threaten you at any time? Claim that you were spying on him? Things like that?'

So much for Wilbur and friend. Shaver heard their door click shut discreetly when he was halfway up the stairs and there was the sound of a bolt sliding before his feet reached the top. Haw, he thought, actually smiling and a short time later, working the celluloid, he caught himself softly whistling.

A very temporary state of affairs. The tune died on his lips the moment Shaver entered the flat. You fool, he thought, cursing himself. You're such a stupid flipping fool. Celebrating a minor skirmish when the major battle is already lost.

Whoever was responsible had done his work well. No

over-turned chairs and fallen lamps or other signs of struggle. There were only three things out of the ordinary in the whole apartment. Puddle of dried blood. Jagged glass of smashed window. Torn curtain flapping on night wind.

Shaver sagged against the wall. What in the hell could this mean? That the Russians had got impatient and taken matters into their own hands?

His mind reeled with the insanity of such a course. The PM screaming mad. Kosygin's visit canceled. A terrible row and diplomatic relations threatened – and his own hide on the rack; stretched, cured, and tanned.

No, Shaver thought. The Russians aren't daft. They daren't do *this*. Or did they?

Six

Petapiece could barely contain his joy. 'Here's the part I like best,' he said, quoting again from the newspaper '"The abductor, who represented himself as being a police officer, was described as having a slightly dazed expression, and authorities reasoned that he might be under the influence of alcohol or drugs." '

'That's me, all right,' Shaver said. 'To a *t*.' He sipped at his cold coffee and wondered what it would take to acquire a more properly alert mien. The streets wouldn't be safe tonight. Everywhere people would be pointing. There he goes! That must be the culprit! See how he looks! Hit in the face with a paddle!

'Here's another drollery,' Petapiece said. ' "The abductor paid two visits to the rooming house. The first time he was driven off by a large yellow tomcat." '

'Wilbur,' Shaver said, jamming his wound in his pocket. He truly was a marked man, he thought. The Mercurochrome Kid. Branded by a 2 per cent aqueous solution of dibromohydroxymercurifluorescein-sodium.

'Wilbur?'

'The beast's name.'

'Oh dear,' Petapiece said, dangerously close to tears. 'I haven't had such a laugh since Suez. Are you always this inept?'

'Only on the important cases.'

Petapiece exploded with pent-up laughter and Shaver felt his face start to color. He was thankful that there were so few other patrons in The Stump Club at this time of morning. Just an elderly couple, the man still half asleep, and that constant presence, the one-handed dart player who fancied himself another Yul Brynner.

'Important, yes,' Petapiece said, finally getting himself

under control. 'Quite so ...' He took a deep breath and folded the newspaper and set it aside. 'There's a lot more to this than meets the eye. Did you ever stop to think how important?'

Shaver took the risk of glancing heavenward. Oh, God, he pleaded. Save me from this grubby idiot. I'm in no mood for a bloody lecture.

'We're leading Uncle Sam by the nose,' Petapiece said, oblivious. 'Remember the first Canadian wheat sales to Russia? The Yanks fairly shat at that. Truck and trade with the enemy.' His gaze moved to the gray sheets in which he found so much pleasure. 'But who's talking business deals in Moscow these days? Henry Ford.'

Shaver nodded dully. Three cheers for our daily newspaper. How else to keep pace with the wild rush of events?

'You see Ottawa's grand design?' Petapiece demanded. 'We keep forcing Washington's hand by our example. First rapport with the Russians. Then with the Red Chinese. And if Ottawa can do it, why not Washington, eh?' The pale blue eyes kindled. 'You know where the world's headed from this small beginning? President Nixon raising his champagne glass in Peking's Great Hall.'

'Cor blimey,' Shaver said. He wondered what was wrong with the dart player. The poor chap's game had really gone to pot. He couldn't even hit the board.

'Mark my words,' Petapiece said. 'The PM knows what he's doing. If this visit goes well, it's Washington next for Kosygin, or perhaps Nixon off to Moscow.' He leaned forward earnestly and though his voice was low it still rang with conviction. 'A whole new era – the superpowers at peace at last – and all your making, eh, lad?'

'Mine?'

'Why not have the credit?' Petapiece asked, smiling. 'If Kosygin meets ill on our fair soil – say a nasty hole in the head – it's back to the bomb shelters for all of us.' He suddenly reached out to grasp and squeeze Shaver's hand. 'But there's no chance of that happening. Not with this big thumb in Henke's eye.'

Shaver sat staring at him solemnly. No one, not even an

officer in the RCMP, could be quite this stupid. The poor man must be daft.

'Resourceful, you are,' Petapiece said. 'You know your business and you'll be doing it right. Henke's fast asleep in some basement room. You're keeping him that way with an injection every few hours . . .' Now his voice was the merest whisper. 'Tell me. Where have you got him stashed?'

Shaver found it difficult to pull his hand free.

'You're right,' Petapiece said. 'It's your dark secret, isn't it? There's no one you dare tell.'

'My sentiments exactly,' Shaver agreed.

Seven

Shaver left The Stump Club wondering how he had managed to carry it off. It was madness, pure madness, and he was in a lot of dire trouble if it didn't work, but it was nevertheless worth the gamble. If he had told Petapiece the truth his career would have been down the drain right then. This way he had two days' grace. Two fleeting days to solve the strange disappearance of Rudolph Henke.

With luck, he just might make it, Shaver thought, dodging across the street to his Plymouth. He'd had the whole night to lay his plans and he'd devised a way to get some help. It was a wild scheme – almost as crazy as the stunt he'd just pulled – but that was appropriate to his destination. He was headed for the Riverview Mental Asylum.

As Shaver drove off, not thinking to look behind, the dart player came out of the club, signaling desperately to a man watching from an upstairs window in one of the office buildings across the street. Moments later they met on the sidewalk in front of the building.

'It doesn't make sense,' the man from the office gasped.

'I gathered that much,' the dart player snarled, slashing at the man with his stump. 'Don't just stand there. We're lost unless we catch him.'

Detective Sergeant Hardison, laughingly referred to as the ace investigator of the Homicide Squad, Vancouver City Police, didn't seem to like the idea at all. 'There's proper channels, you know,' he complained. 'It's all down in black and white in the inspector's office. Privy to them what's got half a business with it.' He signed the admission form and recited his question. 'Why not get it official?'

'I've got a good reason not to.'

'Such as?'

Shaver sighed and looked at the wretched creature Hardison was booking into the asylum. Gnarled fingers were poised impatiently at the jockstrap bulging on the withered crotch. Shaver hoped his expression was clear enough. It's not my habit, Hardison, to discuss matters of state in the presence of sex perverts, and this fellow you have in hand is doubly certifiable.

'Him?' Hardison grumbled. 'You needn't worry. He's crazier than a shithouse rat. Nothing you could say would register – and he's going where no one listens anyhow.'

'A menace removed,' Shaver said. He folded his coat over the back of a chair and placed his cap on top of it. How heartening to have events move so predictably, but then his horoscope had promised as much, hadn't it? *The morning is fine for anything that requires precision. Don't neglect work that is vital to your career. Make plans to improve wardrobe. Be wise.* 'I wish I could say the same thing about your superior.'

'The inspector? Now what the hell is that supposed to mean?'

'What do you think?'

'That I could use another admitting card.'

'Naw,' Shaver said. 'They wouldn't take you here. It's only medium security.' He crossed to the barred window and got out his Sweet Caps. The bigger the lie, they claimed, the easier it went down, and he was trying hard for proof of that these days. 'You were asking why I didn't go through channels. Well, there's your reason, if you must know it.'

'The inspector?' Hardison repeated, incredulous. This, obviously, was blasphemy, and dead ahead were the gates of Hell. 'I've never heard such bloody nonsense.'

'Is it?' Shaver asked softly. 'I fancy a simple visit to headquarters instead of chasing you out to this funny farm – and I don't normally put myself to needless trouble.'

Hardison took a deep breath and exhaled noisily. 'You're serious?'

'What do you think?'

'Well,' Hardison said. He pulled the other chair under him and fell into it like a stone. 'Henke? I don't get the connection . . .' There was a long pause and then the plaintive question surfaced from the depths of his despair. 'Spy stuff?'

'I'm afraid so,' Shaver said. 'It involves the Russians. Breach of the Official Secrets Act . . .' He thought that even in the window you could see the new gray in Hardison's pallor. 'I can't tell you more than that, but my advice is to duck when this one blows, Guy. It's going to be very, very sticky.'

Hardison shook his head. 'O'Brien? I've known him twenty years and he's straight as they come.'

'Be patient,' Shaver counseled. 'You'll have your chance. The defense will be anxious for all the character witnesses they can get. They won't have anything else.' He lit up and blew smoke at the window. 'That's what I like. Loyalty.'

Hardison rallied faintly at that bugle call. Some small succor for a fallen comrade. 'What I told you is the truth. There's nothing I know to incriminate him.'

'Did I ask you that?' Shaver demanded. 'As I recall, I inquired about a routine police matter, which I have a perfect right to do, and you got all mucking officious with me. There'd be no mention of reasons if you'd seen fit to cooperate.'

'That's all you want to know? The results of my investigation?'

'Results?' Shaver said. 'You're suggesting you have some?' He glanced disdainfully at their anxious third party. 'All your time seems taken up with more important matters.'

'It's a favor,' Hardison began, and then changed his mind, but it was obvious who had saddled him with this nonsense.

'To satisfy some of the inspector's friends, eh?'

Hardison was still looking away. 'Yes.'

'That fits,' Shaver said, a hound pouncing on this fortuitous scrap. 'It's a pattern that will continue. You'll get precious little time to go looking for Henke. It's to the inspector's great advantage that the poor devil never be found.'

'We're short staffed . . .'

'So are we,' Shaver said quickly. 'That's why they sent me round to ask your help.' He stubbed out his cigarette on the window sill as if bracing for a plunge. 'It's essential that you give me everything you've got so far. Fact, theory, wild guesses – the works.'

This time there was no hesitation or complaint. 'Sure.'

'And, of course, we wouldn't want O'Brien – or anyone else, for that matter – to learn of this meeting.'

Hardison nodded. 'There's no harm in that, I suppose. You know the old saying. What 'e don't know don't 'urt 'im.'

'A doubtful premise,' Shaver said. 'But this is one occasion where it may have some application.' He left the window and went to stand over the older policeman. 'Have you established any motive for this Henke panky? The vault broken open and the family fortune gone? Milk missing from the fridge?'

'No. You couldn't call it robbery. There was a fair sum of money left behind in plain sight. Plus a few other items no self-respecting cracksman could bring himself to leave.'

'It's a sex crime, then, with semen all over the ceiling, and a whole drawer full of pubic hairs?'

'Hardly,' Hardison laughed. 'You saw his picture in the press? Who could love that? Even from behind?'

Two nurses came in and Shaver abandoned further inquiries. There'd be a short interruption while Hardison's loony played his dirty trick on them. You could tell in advance how they were going to react, Shaver thought. The Jamaican girl, fat and shiny and with that marvelous sing-song voice, would think it a great lark, and the Chinese, thin and mean and very new to the country, or so her accent suggested, would not be amused.

'You have a patients?' the Chinese asked Hardison.

'That one,' he told her, taking the trouble to point.

The Chinese accepted the news without argument. Shaver thought that he was fully dressed, and the other fellow had only his long underwear, and this probably helped a bit.

'Violent?'

'No. Just silly.'

The Chinese put away her hypo – there was a certain reluctance, bred, perhaps, of disappointment – and the loony couldn't wait any longer. He pulled the rubber chicken out of his jockstrap with a marvelous flourish. Only years of practice could so perfect that. 'Would you like to see my cock?' he asked.

The Jamaican girl screamed in delight and clapped her ample thigh and hot tears ran down her black face. The Chinese merely flinched and that was hardly noticeable. Shaver decided she was perfectly suited to her profession. The countenance of a bedpan. 'Is that what brought him here?' he asked.

'Yes,' Hardison said. 'The neighbors found it wearisome after a while.' He got out his pipe and sniffed doubtfully at the bowl. 'But you didn't come to discuss flashing.'

'No. Murder's my game.'

'Murder, is it?' Hardison murmured. He checked to make sure the nurses were properly engrossed in their duties and then took Shaver's place at the window. His tired eyes searched the misty green landscape rolling away toward the river. The activities in the parking lot below made no real impression on his mind. It wasn't his car. He parked elsewhere. 'Where's the body?'

Shaver held his tongue a moment. He mustn't appear too eager. 'You don't think there is one?'

'I don't know,' Hardison said sadly. 'But enough blood was spilled for two corpses. On the living-room rug, down the fire escape, across the backyard. Buckets of it.' He found his tobacco pouch and carefully loosened the sticky tape guarding its aromatic treasures. 'A veritable bloodbath and still the question persists.'

'What's this?' the Chinese wanted to know. She had pulled some old rag from a cardboard valise.

'A nightgown?' the Jamaican proposed.

Hardison turned to look. He saw his duty and did it. 'A nightshirt.'

'One nightshirts,' the Chinese decided. She waited for the Jamaican to accept the ruling – these things must be committed to paper before they can be considered an actual fact – and then snipped two inches off her roll of adhesive and laboriously printed the patient's name on it and stuck it inside the collar of the garment.

'Buckets?'

'Pints then,' Hardison confessed, filling his pipe. 'We think

65

about six. That's a ruddy lot to lose and still survive unless you get medical attention fantastically soon.' He satisfied himself as to depth, firmness, and ease of draw, returned a few excess shreds of tobacco to the pouch, and closed it with the same careful ceremony that had marked the opening. 'Our villains weren't headed for the General, though. If it was medical attention they had in mind, they'd stop the flow first, wouldn't you think? They wouldn't let it spurt out all over the world.'

'Plural?'

'One man could go down a fire-escape ladder carrying a pig the size of Henke? I've obviously put out the wrong description. I should be looking for King Kong.'

The Jamaican's singsong rose in unseemly anger. 'It is so! Ask him.'

The Chinese refused. 'You eat *off* a plates.'

'Dentures,' Hardison told her. He glanced at Shaver and for some reason decided that an explanation was required. 'Extras. He lost them, and had new ones made, and then the first pair turned up.'

'That can happen,' Shaver admitted.

'Two denture,' the Chinese pronounced triumphantly, and the Jamaican's precise penmanship became strangely illegible.

'There's evidence that three were involved,' Hardison said. 'The bloke the cat had a go at and two others who left footprints in the mud in the backyard.'

'You haven't placed the bungler out back?'

'No. We found only size ten prints there. The same as Henke's. From the description, the first bloke was a long, lean one, same as you. Probably size twelves.'

'That's a coincidence, isn't it?' Shaver asked. 'The same size footprints in the mud? Does it suggest anything to you?'

'It did initially,' Hardison said. He searched through his pockets and produced three burned off match stubs before finding a usable one which he lit with his thumbnail.

The compleat smoker, Shaver thought. He marks only himself, and he carries away his mess, and it will be interesting to note if he exhales. 'What changed your mind?'

Hardison stood watching the match go out. 'We found that the heels of the shoes had been worn down differently and that the depressions varied in depth in the same area of ground.'

'So?' Shaver said, offering his lighter. 'What's to stop Henke from buying a couple pairs of old shoes from the Goodwill? What's to prevent him from tramping his back-yard with a sack of coal on his back?'

'Nothing. If he weren't bleeding so bloody hard ...' The lighter snapped shut without the flame appearing. 'You're suggesting that was faked, too?'

'Why not? Did you ever see my impression of a severed artery? The only prop I need is a gravy syringe.'

'Plus six pints of Type B. The same as Henke's.'

'Readily available in fifteen per cent of the population.'

Hardison hesitated with the lighter. 'Did you come look-ing for information? Or did you come to give it?'

'It's not my intent to muddy your crystal waters,' Shaver said. 'But you won't mind admitting if they're none too clear in this case?' He stopped and waited, giving Hardison a chance to light his pipe, but the sergeant was past that now. 'Well?'

'Do I have any real proof that Henke was abducted and/or murdered? Is that the question you're asking?'

'I was coming to it.'

'The answer is no.'

'It's theory next, then,' Shaver said, anxious to be done. 'It's possible that the blood and the footprints and all the rest of it were faked by Henke? It's entirely conceivable that he engineered his own phony disappearance?'

'Perhaps,' Hardison said slowly. 'I told you right at the start. I don't dig no graves unless I first sees the corpse ...' He reached forward and dropped the lighter into Shaver's waiting hand. 'But why would Henke go to such trouble to pull a disappearing act? Why not simply walk away?'

Shaver made no reply. Why indeed? The simple answer, he thought, was that Henke wanted the authorities to think him dead, so that he'd be free to attack Kosygin. But with no corpse, even fools would be suspicious, more on their guard, looking for him to try something. So Henke had called attention to himself, not diverted it, and that didn't make sense, did it?

No, Shaver thought. There was no simple answer to this mess. It was complicated and it was devious and it had him sweating. 'I wish I knew,' he said at last.

'There's another problem, too,' Hardison said. 'You're forgetting the bloke who got it from the cat. If this is a fake disappearance – how do you explain him?'

Shaver shrugged. 'Henke's accomplice?'

There was a bit of a wait. 'Interesting . . .'

'Your kind of a case,' Shaver said. 'Despite other priorities, I'd devote all my time to this one, Guy. Finding Henke for us could prove quite a plume in your helmet.' He took out a card and passed it. 'But don't tell the inspector if you do. Tell me.'

'It's the rule,' the Chinese insisted shrilly. She dug into the jockstrap and got a firm grip on the chicken's head. She pulled and the loony held fast and the neck stretched dangerously.

'Oh, fine,' Shaver said, edging away. 'You could lose an eye when that pops. Does she have to take it from him?'

'Them are the regulations,' Hardison said. 'No personal effects in the wards. And besides, if I know this place, they'll be serving it for dinner come Sunday.' His mouth curled in what might be taken for a smile. 'I meant to ask you. Where'd you get the war wound?'

'It weren't from no cat,' Shaver assured him. 'If that's what you were thinking . . .' He got his coat and cap from the back of the chair. 'Remember now. Not a word to anyone.'

The loony let go and the Chinese staggered back and crashed heavily against the wall. She held there a moment, the breath knocked out of her, and then she slowly sank out of sight behind the bed, a scuttled ship settling to the bottom.

Hardison bent over and retrieved her trophy. His face was again blank as he piled it with the rest of the stuff. 'One rubber chickens,' he told the Jamaican.

Shaver went out wondering about him. Was this someone else smarter than he had imagined?

Eight

The dart player, who in reality was a colonel, and who expected to be a general before the week was through, said good-by very softly. He stuck the telephone receiver between his stump and his stomach and held it pinned there a moment and then gently eased it onto the cradle. His heavy, blunt face, which had been flushed with rage such a short time ago, was now placid and smiling. He took a cigarette from a pack of Camels and lit it with a gold-filled Zippo.

'Good news?' asked his subordinate, a plain-looking man whose code name was Samuel.

The colonel nodded dreamily. 'Yes. Our import is there now. They'll have him soon.'

'Good,' Samuel said. There were no words to express his relief. He would be crying with joy if he was alone.

The colonel pulled open a desk drawer and got out a tumbler and a bottle of Dickel's Tennessee Sour Mash Whiskey. He tucked the glass between his stump and his stomach – holding it as he had done with the telephone – and poured himself about two inches. He put the bottle away without offering any to the other man. 'Here's looking at you.'

'Bottoms up,' Samuel said.

The colonel began pacing back and forth in front of the office windows. Every minute or so he'd stop at one of the windows and stare out across the street at The Stump Club. Then he'd smile and shake his head and resume his pacing.

Samuel sat without moving.

'The nerve of the cunt,' the colonel said at last, finishing off his drink. 'Twenty years in the business and I never saw the like. Jesus, what gall.'

'Incredible,' Samuel agreed.

The colonel sat down and rolled his empty glass across the desk so that it bumped against the tape recorder. 'This will stand as a classic,' he decided. 'The stuff of legends. Timeless . . .' He got another cigarette and held it poised at his thick lips. 'Play it again, Sam.'

'Sure,' Samuel said. He turned on the tape recorder.

Shaver bought a small stuffed owl at the asylum's tuck shop. It had been made by a patient and had the peculiar charm of bearing absolutely no relation whatsoever to reality. The perfect gift for Bogna. Something to help him get that F-I-L-E.

Henke's secret file had taken on epic proportions in Shaver's mind ever since his tortured decision to hide the truth of the Latvian's disappearance. Shaver was sure now that Bogna had been telling the truth – that she had relented and done the favor he'd asked – and he also felt that the file might somehow hold the secret to the whole damn puzzle. Why, for example, had Petapiece been so quick to deny the thing to him? – and why had Bogna found it so amusing?

Why? Good questions, both of them, Shaver thought, and his next job was to find the answers. He put the stuffed owl in his raincoat pocket and placed his call from the tuck shop pay phone. He admonished himself to mind his manners and be careful not to rouse her and to hold his own temper no matter what difficulties she decided to present. It wouldn't do for him to hang up again in a pique.

'Hello, luv,' Bogna exclaimed, even more delighted than before. 'I can't believe my good fortune. Two calls in as many days. Are you sure you have your faculties?'

'I'm out at Riverview,' Shaver began.

'Oh,' Bogna said. 'That explains it. You finally admitted yourself, eh?' She laughed rather longer than was necessary. 'Are you allowed visitors? Could I bring you something? How about some smokes? Sweets Caps, aren't they?'

'If you're through, I'll state my purpose,' Shaver told her, already wavering. 'I've got some free time and was just wondering. Could we get together for a bite?'

'Why, sure,' Bogna said. 'I'd be ever so grateful. I'll pick up some chops going home – and could you try to make it by seven?'

Oh, God, Shaver thought. Could anyone imagine her

being so rotten? And he'd never done anything to warrant it, either. 'I meant lunch.'

'*Lunch!*' Bogna swooned. The phone clattered on her desk and there was a babble of voices. 'Stand back!' 'Give her air.' 'Has anyone called an ambulance?'

'You've had your fun?' Shaver said after a while. 'Could you take time out to give me your answer? Yes or no?'

His anger only provoked more laughter. 'It depends when. You know how heavily I'm booked. But there has been a cancellation in January.'

'It's something special I've in mind,' Shaver said, prepared to sacrifice. 'Get a table for us at the Dev. I can just make it by noon if I run.'

'The Carriage Room?' Bogna asked. The sudden change in her tone was remarkable. 'I don't think I'm quite dressed for that. I wish you'd warned me.'

Sure, Shaver thought. He would have, had this part been planned, but as it was, he'd have to borrow a tie himself. 'Come on. You're good enough, and the chef's a genius there. Have you ever had mustard-glazed carrots?'

'No.'

'Then prepare for a treat.'

'All right,' she agreed. 'I'll meet you in the lobby. A bit after twelve . . .' She sat puzzled for a moment and then decided she simply had to ask. 'Where did *you* ever have mustard-glazed carrots?'

'Well,' Shaver said, 'you probably won't believe this, but I've had them on my elbows.' It was time to ring off. 'You won't forget that F-I-L-E?'

There was a hurt pause. Nothing Bogna could help or explain. She had known his motive since first hearing his voice. 'I won't,' she replied stiffly.

'Thank you,' Shaver said. It was his turn to laugh and he thought that this was another of Bogna's saving graces. She could accept the truth when it was rammed down her throat.

The Stump Club's day-shift bartender cupped a hand over the telephone and called across the room in a harsh stage whisper. 'Are you here?'

Petapiece nodded.

'He's here,' the bartender said. He stretched the phone cord its full limit and hung the receiver over the far edge of the bar. Then he went back to washing glasses.

Petapiece finished the last of his drink and put his newspaper back together in the proper order before getting up from his table. He took much longer than necessary crossing the room and made a point of knocking the telephone against the bar as he picked it up. 'Your nickel,' he said gaily.

The bartender held a glass up to the light. There was something funny going on, he thought. The old mooch had just bought his first round in history and now he was putting on this show. It must be an historic occasion.

'I hardly thought it necessary to call,' Petapiece said, laughing. 'It's all there in your morning paper, and on the front page, too.'

The bartender decided the chip wasn't that bad after all and put the glass aside to dry. There's more to the man than meets the eye, he thought. The telephone calls coming all through the day and the strangers always visiting at his table. It was something the coppers ought to look at.

'A bit messy, sure,' Petapiece said. 'But it's the results that count, isn't it?' He signaled to the bartender that he could use another ale. 'I've no complaints myself – and I doubt that yours are much valid.'

The bartender got the bottle and snapped it open and left it next to the cash register. He'd be damned if he'd make special deliveries to that suspicious character. The man was as sneaky as they come.

'Listen,' Petapiece said tiredly, his gay mood fast disappearing. 'You wanted it done and it's done. There's no turning back now.' He lowered his voice and turned to face the other way. 'This is a fine time to start getting cold feet.'

The bartender stood listening and wondering. He really ought to call the coppers, he thought. It wouldn't do no harm.

'One question,' Petapiece said. 'What exactly are you proposing? That we put Humpty-Dumpty together again?' He smiled at the answer he got and then posed another question. 'Well, what is it that you *do* want?'

The bartender told himself that he ought to take notes. They might be needed as evidence.

'Fine by me,' Petapiece said. 'I couldn't agree more. Nothing is what I do best.' He put the phone back and let out his breath in a long noisy wheeze. That was so typical of the bum boys upstairs, he thought. Always second guessing. Always running scared.

'There's your ale,' the bartender said.

'You have it,' Petapiece told him. He went back to his table for his coat and strode angrily out of the club.

The bartender stood drinking the ale. He told himself that this was all very suspicious and there wasn't one good reason why he shouldn't call the coppers.

Shaver saw his Plymouth dangling from a tow truck's hoist as he pushed out the front door of the admissions office at Riverview. He shook his head in disbelief and ran down the stairs shouting but the driver couldn't hear with the truck's windows closed.

'Hey!' Shaver cried. 'You there! Hey ...!' He stopped at the foot of the stairs, despairing of catching up, and then changed his mind and broke into a hard run, headed for the parking lot exit. The truck had a long head start but it had a couple of tight turns to make in the lot before reaching the exit. He just might be able to cut it off.

Shaver dashed madly along the slippery road, wasting his breath swearing, and convinced that he'd fall and break a leg any moment. But he had to stop the truck, he thought. He couldn't afford the delay of getting his car out of impoundment – and the taxi bills without it were too much to comprehend.

The truck eased out of the lot, the driver unaware that he was being chased, and Shaver put on one final desperate spurt, managing to slam his fist against the trunk of his car as he collapsed.

Why this? Shaver wondered, staring helplessly at the departing vehicles. It never failed but your troubles all came together. One at a time and there'd be fewer suicides.

The truck driver glanced belatedly in his rear view mirror – he'd heard metal banging somewhere – and saw Shaver sprawled on the road. His first thought was that he had knocked someone down and his first impulse was to keep on going. But then his eyes moved to the many rows of windows in the buildings behind him and he decided that wasn't so wise. He swore and stopped the truck.

Shaver slowly got to his feet.

'You all right?' the truck driver called. He had opened his door and was standing on the running board.

'No,' Shaver said, the one word all he could get out. He hadn't run that fast in years and his lungs were burning.

'You fall or something?' the truck driver asked. He had made up his mind not to admit responsibility.

Shaver didn't want to answer until he was sure he had breath enough. He made it to his car, and leaned against the hood.

'Well?' the truck driver demanded. 'What the hell's the matter? You drunk or something?'

'It's my car,' Shaver managed.

'Yours?'

'Yes,' Shaver said softly. 'It's mine, and you can put it back.' This was so like the cheeky tow bastards, he thought. They're caught stealing your car and they're asking you questions.

'Back?'

'Back.'

'Great,' the driver said. 'I ought to have known. A nut.' He reached in the cab for his clipboard and then jumped down off the running board. 'I suppose you never called in and asked for a tow?'

'Back,' Shaver repeated. There really wasn't the time, nor was he up to it, but this still might end in a brawl, he decided. The bastard was asking for it.

'We made this all up, then?' the driver demanded, shoving the clipboard at him.

Shaver's anger cooled when he read it. No wonder the driver was chippy. He had the correct car and he was only doing as instructed. Twenty minutes before, someone had phoned his firm, giving the license number and location, and asking that it be towed to a garage for repairs.

'Someone's idea of a joke,' Shaver said, passing back the board. 'I'm sorry if you're inconvenienced, but there's nothing I can do about it, I'm afraid. I'm equally the victim.'

'A joke?'

'You're not amused?' Shaver asked. 'Well, nor am I.' He got out his keys and motioned brusquely. 'Get the damn thing unhooked, will you? I'm late for an appointment.'

'Who's going to pay?'

'Pay what?'

'What the hell do you think?' the driver asked. 'There's a minimum charge for bringing out the goddam truck. Seven-fifty.'

'Is there?' Shaver put the keys back in his pocket and got himself set. There was going to be a brawl, all right, and the sad part was that he had to lose, because the last thing he wanted now was to keep the car. That would spoil everything. 'You've got exactly five seconds to start unhooking the thing. Then you've got a dental bill to worry about.'

The driver stared incredulously. 'I beg your fucking pardon?'

'Four seconds.'

'Well,' the driver said, grinning. 'I was hoping I heard you right.' He flung aside his clipboard and advanced eagerly. 'We'll see whose teeth get loosened.'

Shaver's left hand exploded in a long looping arc and he hit the driver in the face very hard and full-on and split his lower lip for him. He sighed contentedly and rolled away along the side of the Plymouth. His best punch and he had gotten it off perfectly. The same way he'd done it to McDermott.

'You pig fucker,' the driver screamed, enraged. He wiped the blood from his mouth and charged blindly.

Shaver hit him in the face again with same looping left, closing an eye this time, and a hard right chop followed an instant later, banging like a hammer against the temple.

The driver staggered and went down to his knees.

'Seriously,' Shaver said, rolling away. 'Unhook the car. Otherwise I'll cut you to pieces.'

The driver pushed very slowly to his feet. He felt his

temple and then his eye and then his lip. 'A professional, huh?'

'Not really,' Shaver said. 'I've never been paid. Except by way of pleasure.'

'You really like to push it, don't you, Mac?' the driver said. 'I was thinking of shaking hands. But not with a prick.' He edged backward to the cab of his truck and reached under the seat and pulled out a tire iron. 'You want your car? Come and get it.'

Shaver unbuttoned his raincoat. He didn't stand a chance against that blunt-edged sword and he was far too tired to run.

'You don't want it?' the driver taunted.

'I guess not,' Shaver said.

'It'll be waiting at our yard,' the driver told him, swinging up into the cab. 'If you change your mind, you just drop around and get it, Mac. It'll be waiting for you there. That and a lot more.'

Shaver stood watching the truck take his car away – he congratulated himself on how well its departure had been arranged – and then decided to go back to the parking lot. There ought to be someone about with an offer of assistance, he thought. Some providential Good Samaritan.

'Say,' a voice called, as if on cue, and Shaver turned to see a well-rubbed Rover sedan silently gliding toward him. The car pulled alongside and the man at the wheel examined him with a strangely pained expression. 'You've had a spot of trouble?'

'A misunderstanding,' Shaver said, smiling. He'd never seen such a dandy, he thought. A small white carnation in the lapel and gray chamois gloves. The man could hire out as a professional mourner. Especially with those sad eyes.

'I'm going into town,' the dandy said. 'I could drop you off . . .' He colored slightly for no apparent reason. 'I take it you'll be calling at the police station?'

Well, Shaver thought. Wasn't this fortuitous? He'd always wanted a run in a Rover 3500 V-8. 'It's on your way?'

'Yes.'

Shaver crossed in front of the gleaming car and slid in beside his benefactor and smiled again when he saw the spats. They were too much, really, but then so was the rest of him, frail to the point of being dainty, and wearing an aftershave lotion you could only buy at a perfume counter.

'You're quite good with your fists,' the dandy noted, his moist eyes falling on Shaver's clasped hands.

Shaver wondered what he had here? A fight promoter? 'You saw that, did you?'

'A witness if you want,' the dandy said, a small surge of red coloring his cheeks. He let out the clutch and the Rover slid away like ice cream melting on a cone. 'I heard what he called you. Some people are animals.'

'A dirty mouth,' Shaver agreed. He examined the interior of the car appreciatively and saw a black leather satchel sitting on the back seat. 'You work here, I take it? A psychiatrist?'

'Yes. But only on a consulting basis. I'm called in when they want advice on releases.'

'Spreading the blame?'

The dandy frowned in answer, a pinched, hurt look, and concentrated on his driving. Two swift turns and they were through the gates of the asylum and on their way, the Rover's V-8 faintly audible now, the Avon radials humming on the asphalt.

'What mad killer was sprung today?' Shaver asked.

'That's not,' the dandy began, and then his face softened. Up ahead, there was a Chrysler off the road, its hood raised in the international distress signal, and two men were staring haplessly at the innards. 'This seems to be my day for rescue missions. You don't mind if I stop?'

'You couldn't be more wrong,' Shaver said. He put his Webley in his benefactor's ear and pressed hard enough to hurt. 'If you stop, I'll blow your brains out, chum. They'll never fit them back.'

'What's this?'

'A gun.'

The dandy nodded tightly – Shaver wondered at how well he accepted the bad news – and suddenly they were doing sixty. The stranded pair watched in disbelief as they went flying by. One of them, a huge, hulking giant of a man, seemed particularly shattered. This wasn't in the script.

'Faster,' Shaver ordered. He edged back against his door and chose a lower target for the Webley. 'The manual says this exquisite piece of machinery will do one hundred and eighteen. Don't argue with it.'

The dandy nodded again and pressed the accelerator to the floor and then eased off just enough to keep them on the road. 'Which way?'

'East. There's not much traffic.'

'Any particular place in mind?'

'Not yet. It all depends.'

Shaver reached into the back seat and got the satchel. The rear window framed two distant figures slamming down the hood of the Chrysler. Strange they should fix it so promptly. 'There's just the three of you?'

'Yes.'

'You wouldn't lie to me?'

'No.'

I'll bet, Shaver thought. The satchel opened to reveal a consulting psychiatrist's usual stock of goodies. A coil of heavy twine. A fat roll of adhesive. A hypodermic with the needle imbedded in a rubber cork.

'This, now,' Shaver said holding up the hypo. 'What would happen if I jabbed it in your arm?'

The dandy licked at dry lips. 'You'd have to take the wheel rather suddenly.'

Ah yes, Shaver thought, you meet the nicest guys at River-view. He put the hypo back and returned the satchel to the rear seat. There was no sense keeping it within easy reach. The temptation to use it might prove irresistible. 'You want to tell me who you're working for?'

'I'd be happy to,' the dandy said, 'if I knew.' He slowed the car for the junction looming ahead. 'But the fact of the matter is I don't.'

Shaver waited for him to negotiate the sharp turn onto the highway – he did it perfectly, decelerating just enough, and hardly any skid at all – and then reached into the man's pocket and removed his wallet. 'You just blindly follow orders?'

'Providing the fee is high enough.'

Shaver flipped through the wallet. Jamie Cardigani, supposedly, and he came from Detroit, of all places, and he didn't use credit cards. 'This really you?'

'Yes.'

'Imported, for Christ's sake?'

'Only the best.'

Shaver glanced out the rear window. The dandy's friends still hadn't made it onto the highway. Sometimes the best just isn't good enough, Shaver thought. If they were really good, this wouldn't be the fastest car, now would it?

'When did you get the contract?'

'A few days back.'

'Anything special they wanted done?'

'No. Just a plain funeral.'

Shaver put the wallet back and patted around until he found a hipholster and removed a Smith & Wesson Combat .357 Magnum. A big gun for such a small man. He'd sprain his fist firing. 'What's my head worth these days anyhow?'

'Thirty thousand. Half in advance.'

Shaver whistled softly and stuck the Combat in his belt. It would take him over two years to earn that much, he thought, and that was counting the tips, too. 'Anything else I should know?'

'Yes. You're awfully lucky.'

Shaver smiled. Now wasn't that the truth? Just a couple of minutes more would have made all the difference. If the tow truck driver had been gone with his car, he probably would have walked smiling into the trap, thanking this sweet-smelling petunia for the ride.

Urged on by the Webley, the dandy pushed the car harder, the speedometer tapping at 120 on the straight runs, the tires squealing in agony on the curves, and soon his partners-in-crime were left far behind. To be truthful, he hadn't met much better, Shaver thought. One hell of a driver.

'Slow down,' Shaver said after a while. 'You'll turn off at the next right. There's a road winding down to the river and a railroad crossing at the bottom of the hill. You'll turn left there, onto the railway right-of-way, and you'll drive along the tracks themselves, crossing the trestle over the river.'

The dandy's expression changed for the first time since he'd been caught out. The fear that never fails to show in a condemned man's eyes. Shaver almost felt sorry for him for a moment. Had he actually thought he'd go directly to jail in this game?

'The river?'

'Yes,' Shaver said. 'The mighty Fraser. You're going in unless I hear who hired you and why.'

'I said I don't know.'

'We'll see.'

They reached the bottom of the hill and turned off onto the railway right-of-way and bounced along the ties to the trestle. The dandy slowed there, the point of no return, and then, gently prodded by the Webley, took the Rover out over the middle of the river.

'This'll do,' Shaver said. 'It's fast and deep here. And icy cold . . .' He waited for the car to come to a complete stop and for the hand brake to be set and then he reached over and took possession of the keys. 'Did you happen to bring your trunks?'

The dandy opened his door without being asked – he was strangely resigned now, and even anxious to get it done, perhaps? – and went and stood in front of the car. Shaver followed him out and motioned with the Webley, and the dandy moved to the edge of the trestle and stared down bleakly at the rushing water.

'Well?' Shaver asked.

'How many times do I have to tell you?' the dandy said, still looking at the water. 'I don't know who or why. They never say in this business.'

'Come on, chum,' Shaver said, aiming at his head. 'Your last chance now. Fink or swim.'

The dandy's eyes moved to meet Shaver's – they were moist once more, but for a different reason, Shaver thought – and then he suddenly let himself go. There was a muffled cry and a splash as he hit and that's all. The river took him and he was gone.

Shaver lowered the gun and stood staring dumbly at the swirling current. It wasn't supposed to turn out this way. The man was no good to him dead.

There was proof of his good intentions, Shaver thought. The dear little perfumed darling had a pocketbook stuffed with cash. If he was really going to kill the dear, he'd have kept it, wouldn't he?

Nine

Bogna slammed into her office and threw her coat on her desk and tore open the stale cheese sandwich that had been the last offering at the blind vendor's stand. She bit into it viciously and swallowed without chewing properly. Her eyes were wet with angry tears.

One of the filing clerks tapped on the glass divider wall that separated her small cubbyhole from the rest of the Records Section. The girl pointed and mouthed the words. *You saw that message?*

Bogna put the sandwich aside and took the message off the spike. She tore it into small pieces and threw the shreds in the wastepaper basket. The clerk stared dumbly for a moment and then hurriedly returned to her work.

The phone rang a few minutes later. Bogna threw away what remained of her sandwich before picking it up. She noted the little extra ring on the line that signified an outside call and she waited for the caller to identify himself.

'Miss Kirchoff,' Bogna replied icily, her voice strained to the point of breaking, 'is not accepting calls from Corporal Shaver.' Then she hung up.

This performance was repeated three more times in the next hour and did not vary so much as by a word.

The colonel was watching from his office window as Peta-piece strode out of The Stump Club. Samuel, standing beside him, uttered a small cry of dismay. 'Do you want him followed?'

The colonel shook his head no. He had conquered his anger and he was thinking clearly now and he knew he must conserve his forces. All his efforts must be concentrated on taking the strangely elusive primary objective.

Samuel couldn't hide the doubt he felt.

'It's a question of priorities,' the colonel lectured. 'Corporal Shaver is far more important to us than Petapiece. We might be able to manage without the commander. But Shaver? He's indispensable.'

Samuel nodded. They must find Shaver, of course. He was not only indispensable, he was very, very dangerous. Shaver could turn the whole operation into a shambles if he wasn't run to ground soon. But it also would be wise to protect their flanks and keep a sharp eye on Petapiece.

'Priorities,' the colonel repeated, smiling. 'You must learn priorities. You'll never make a general unless you know your priorities.'

Samuel nodded again. He wasn't inclined to argue, but no one could stop him from thinking, and he wasn't the only one who might not make general, he thought. The colonel might not make it either.

'I'm glad you agree.'

Samuel felt his face about to redden. He decided it would be best to change the subject. 'The phone call was a good sign,' he said.

The colonel was still smiling. 'Wasn't it?'

Shaver banged down the phone and drained the cup of bitter poison which passed for coffee at the Vancouver Police Department's Crime Laboratory.

'She still won't talk to you?' Manoocher asked needlessly.

'Women,' Shaver said, mashing the cardboard container. He told himself there was no sense making any further attempts on the telephone. He'd have to catch her at home after work.

'Then you won't mind taking this call?' Manoocher asked, holding up the other telephone. 'Remind me to requisition a secretary. Especially for you.'

'Who is it?'

'Your pal at the Motor Vehicles Branch.'

Shaver took the phone wordlessly and Manoocher went to answer the knock at his office door. He sometimes wished that the Mounties would get their own crime lab in Vancouver. He was busy enough without them always asking favors.

'Don't worry about the pronunciation,' Shaver told his caller. 'Just tell me how to spell it.' He copied down the jumble of letters and ended up with Bjsgrkowski. Norman Bjsgrkowski. Surely someone was pulling his leg?

'Do you want his address?' he was asked.

'Sure,' Shaver said. This deep into the fairy tale, he might as well hear the ending, he thought. The part where Bjsgrkowski flies home to Saturn.

'It says 1226 Angus Drive.'

'In Shaughnessy, huh?' Shaver said, laughing bitterly. 'I should have guessed. The name fairly reeks of Anglo-Saxon aristocracy.' He looked for it in the telephone book and drew the expected blank. 'You've got a city directory, haven't you? Could you check it out there?'

There was a long wait – Manoocher had returned from the door and was standing by impatiently – and then the Motor Vehicles clerk came back on the phone confused and apologetic. 'This is funny. There must be some mistake. Angus Drive numbers don't start until the 1400 block.'

Hilarious, Shaver thought, somehow failing to see the humor. He made a note of the other information on the Rover's registration form and then hung up and considered destroying all telephones. They were evil instruments which brought him only misfortune and pain.

'You ready for this?' Manoocher asked, passing the analysis on the contents of the hypo. 'It's Ketamine. The stuff dreams are made of.'

'Ketamine?'

'That's right,' Manoocher said. 'Ketamine. The successor to Sodium Pentothal.' He sat down at his desk and poured himself a cup of the coffee. 'Why so surprised? You were expecting some sort of knockout drops, weren't you?'

'I'm not surprised,' Shaver lied. 'It says the hypo contained one thousand milligrams. Is that enough to kill a man?'

Manoocher shook his head. 'No just put them to sleep. They'd go out pretty quick, mind you, but it's really nothing more than a guaranteed cure for insomnia.'

Shaver wondered. Was the drug meant for him? Or had it been intended for someone else and had the dandy been diverted at the last moment? The latter, more likely, he thought. He didn't fit as the sleeping beauty in this fairy tale. He figured much better as a plain corpse.

There was another knock on the door, and a young lab technician in a long white smock entered without waiting for permission. His expression indicated he was pleased about something.

'Bad news?' Shaver asked.

'It's clean, all right,' the youth reported. 'We've been over it twice and there simply aren't any fingerpints.' He looked at Manoocher and then at Shaver. 'Except the couple of places you said you touched and they did turn out to be yours.'

Shaver accepted the rebuff without protest. He had needed some reason for the examination and his story was that the Rover was believed stolen and had possibly been used in the commission of a serious crime. So the lad had a right to expect him to bring the thing in free of his own paw marks.

'How about the parking stub?' Manoocher asked.

'Clean,' the youth repeated, sounding like a detergent salesman. He dug into his smock and handed an envelope to Manoocher. 'Will that be all?'

'Unless you found a million dollars in the trunk,' Manoocher said. He waited for the youth to leave and then passed the envelope to Shaver. 'What's the problem with the registered owner?'

Shaver opened the envelope and took out the ticket he had found in the Rover's glove compartment. It was a receipt for parking at Vancouver International Airport and was the one small shred of evidence that supported the dandy's story about being imported from the United States.

'Well?'

'It's registered to a Norman Bjsgrkowski,' Shaver said, slurring valiantly. 'The only trouble is, that's a phony name, and there's a phony address to go with it.'

Manoocher's eyebrows went up. 'Fake registration? That's kind of dumb ...' He stopped and considered. 'I'm getting lost. Was the heap stolen or not?'

'It looks like not,' Shaver admitted. 'It hasn't been on the road long enough to be stolen. The notice of sale only just got filed with the Motor Vehicles Branch.'

'I am lost.'

Shaver wondered if he should attempt an explanation. Being lost was not an unusual state for Manoocher. His main claim to fame, before they put him in the Crime Lab, was that he'd gone to investigate a motel murder, and the killer was waiting there in the room, and Manoocher sent him out to call for an ambulance, which the chap very kindly did – only he didn't come back.

'It's simple enough,' Shaver said, fingering the parking receipt. 'This Bjsgrkowski character purchased the Rover from British Motor Imports last Tuesday. He parked it that very same day at Vancouver International Airport, and it remained there until this morning.'

Manoocher looked more bewildered than ever. 'When it *wasn't* stolen?'

'When it was picked up as arranged,' Shaver said. 'Try this theory on for size: Bjsgrkowski wants a certain someone killed and money is no object. He goes first class by contracting for a button man out of Detroit. In the States, the killer would handle his own transportation requirements, but this is a foreign country and he's a bit out of his depth, so he asks his employer to provide him with a good, fast, reliable car. Bjsgrkowski agrees. He buys a Rover and leaves it parked at the airport. Then he sends the parking receipt to the killer along with his down payment and the killer picks up the Rover when he flies in from Detroit.'

'Are you leaving out much?'

'A bit.'

'A lot,' Manoocher decided. 'Something happens to you cowboys when you get assigned to the CIB. The shock of leaving your horse . . .' He took a thick finger and twirled it at his temple. 'Wouldn't it be just as simple – and a whole lot cheaper – to rent a car?'

'They required something fast. Capable of doing about one hundred and twenty. And have you ever tried asking Hertz for a Rover?'

'Oh,' Manoocher said. He thought about that awhile and came to the conclusion he was being treated unfairly. 'If you already know all the answers, why come asking me, for Christ's sake?'

Oh sure, Shaver thought. He had all the answers, all right. All the answers except the important ones. Such as who did Bjsgrkowski originally have in mind for a funeral when he bought the Rover for that sweet-smelling darling from Detroit? It sure as hell wasn't yours truly, Shaver thought. The Rover had been purchased on Tuesday – and it wasn't until the next day that he got the assignment from Petapiece.

'What about the car?' Manoocher asked. 'It's not stolen, but you don't know who owns it. You got an answer for that?'

'Sure,' Shaver said tiredly. 'I ran into exactly the same situation on one of my first cases. It was an alleged house-breaking but there was no sign of forced entry and nothing had been stolen.'

'So why call the police?'

'That's what I said,' Shaver said. 'So the owner of the place takes me into the bathroom and shows me the toilet bowl and asks me what's in it. A turd, I says, and the chap says a piece of shit, and we're agreed on that part, and it turns out that he didn't do it and his wife didn't and neither did his mother-in-law and that's why he wants an investigation.'

'You're kidding . . .'

'Uh-uh,' Shaver said. He got his coat and cap and started for the door. 'Well, I says, I can't initiate no investigation with just a turd to go on, but the chap is insistent and there's a big argument and he follows me out onto the street shouting, What about this turd? So I stops to think for a moment and finally the answer comes to me. Keep it for seven days, I says, and if nobody claims it, the thing is yours.'

The colonel concentrated on planning his next move very slowly and carefully. He had almost reaped disaster by the morning's haste and he wouldn't be stampeded again. Mistakes weren't allowed in his profession.

Corporal Shaver was like a grasshopper, he thought. You could never tell which way he was going to jump. The net had to be strung full circle.

Samuel and two other men, the pair who had been teamed with the dandy at Riverview, sat on the other side of the colonel's desk, quietly waiting for his orders. The huge ox of a man went by the code name of Goliath. His partner was known as Kavinsky.

The minutes ticked by for what seemed an eternity. The only sounds were those of the men breathing, and the occasional footsteps in the hall, and the faint hum of the traffic from the street below.

'It's the corporal's overdeveloped instinct for survival that presents the problem,' the colonel said at last. 'Our stakeouts have failed because he has no intention of going to his superiors. He's still playing for time and trying to solve the puzzle on his own. He knows this is the only way to save his neck and he'll probably keep on trying until the last possible moment.'

The threesome on the other side of the desk nodded as one man.

'I propose to change our tactics,' the colonel said. 'Instead of waiting, we'll go to him, and we'll take him where we find him.' He paused to consider assignments and decided that the first should go to Goliath. 'You'll take the Polack slut's flat. I've got a strange feeling about our grasshopper. I think his next jump will land him there.'

Goliath nodded happily and the colonel thought that a good general had to know his troops and their limitations – how to make latrine duty sound like leading a charge. If he could do that, he was a good general, and this was a perfect example, he thought. There was very little chance of finding Corporal Shaver at the Polish slut's flat. Yet the giant was happy in his work.

The sales manager of British Motor Imports sat with his elbows on his desk and with his fingers forming a church steeple. It was a minor point, but one worth making, he decided. One couldn't be too careful when talking to the police. 'If it's all the same with you, we don't use the term secondhand,' said the sales manager, whose name was Battestin. 'We prefer pre-owned.'

Shaver sighed and made the correction in his notebook.

He told himself it was no wonder that the empire had been lost.

'That, as I've said, was Monday,' Battestin went on, striving to be precise in every detail. 'Mr. Bjsgrkowski returned the next day, Tuesday, with a certified check for the exact amount, including taxes, license, and registration fee. Everything was in order and he took immediate delivery.'

'He paid by check, did he?' Shaver asked, surprised at this disclosure. It seemed a rather novel method of obtaining a car to be used in a contract murder. 'Do you recall which bank?'

Battestin nodded. 'The Royal. Main branch. I telephoned them to make doubly sure. It was a rather large sum, after all, and we'd had no previous dealings with the gentleman.'

'The bank knew him well?'

'It said his check was good. That was my only interest.'

Shaver sighed again and made another entry in his notebook. Bjsgrkowski, he decided, had been wise to pay by certified check, because that was the normal method of auto purchase. Pulling more than three thousand dollars in cash out of his pocket would raise eyebrows and cause him to be particularly remembered. How much simpler to first deposit the money in a bank, a transaction which the teller would have completely forgotten by now, especially at a busy main branch.

'Anything else?'

'Just a description of Bjsgrkowski,' Shaver said. 'The salesman who handled the deal – do you think I might have a chat with him?'

Battestin shook his head. 'I'm sorry. He's on vacation. Off somewhere on a hunting trip.'

'Oh,' Shaver said. He could feel events conspiring. 'Any chance of me reaching him by telephone?'

'None, I fear. He's the type who just disappears into the bush. Won't come out again until he's got his moose.'

'When's he due back at work?'

'Monday.'

'Then what about you?' Shaver asked half-heartedly. 'You say you saw him at a distance when he first looked at the car. Did you see him again when the deal was closed?'

'Not firsthand. He remained in the salesman's office when his check was brought to me for approval. So I didn't get much more than a couple of passing glimpses.'

'But you can provide us with some sort of description?'

'Well,' Battestin said, his steeple collapsing. 'That's going to be a bit difficult. It's been well over a week and we get so many people in and out.' He frowned at what he obviously considered an imposition. 'They all seem to mesh after a while.'

'Even a general idea of his appearance would help.'

'Give me time to think,' Battestin complained. He clasped his hands together again, the two index fingers joined and pointing, a pistol keeping further questions at bay. 'Medium height.'

'Medium height,' Shaver repeated, writing it down. Here it was at last, he thought. Something to go on. 'Did you notice anything else?'

'Average build.'

'And?' Shaver urged, marveling at his luck. The man was uncanny. Total recall.

'Middle-aged.'

'And?'

'An ordinary sort of face.'

'Thank you,' Shaver said. He snapped his notebook shut and put away his pen. 'We'll get a bulletin out immediately. Should have him picked up in no time.'

Battestin's cheeks colored. He unclasped his hands and took his elbows off his desk and looked away in embarrassment. 'I'm afraid I'm not being of much help . . .'

Shaver smiled unhappily. On television, the witness spent five minutes with a police artist and presto! an exact likeness. He wished he might someday meet such a witness. Just once.

'. . . am I?'

'No,' Shaver admitted. He was ready to quit but told himself his only hope lay with Battestin. The bank was going to be a dead end. X number of dollars deposited and X number withdrawn. 'Surely you remember something specific about the man's face? Was it fat or thin? A big nose? Bad teeth?'

'I'm sorry,' Battestin said helplessly. 'If he walked in the door now, I'd recognize him, I guess. But to attempt to describe him?' His shoulders hunched. 'He was just your average chap.'

'Surely something stands out?' Shaver persisted. 'Something that set him apart? A scar? A hearing aid? Perhaps a certain type of glasses?'

'No,' Battestin said. 'The best I can say is that he had a bland face. There was nothing about him that would make a person think to look twice.'

The faceless man, Shaver thought, defeated. He wondered if the bastard had been purposely chosen for his ability to blend with the crowd. That was a handy bloke to have around if you were planning a political assassination.

Detective Sergeant Hardison got out his reverse directory and checked the two telephone numbers. Shaver, Timothy, was listed for the first, and the second was Kirchoff, Bogna, Shaver's lady friend, no doubt.

Home telephone numbers, Hardison thought, frowning. No wonder he hadn't been able to get an answer. The damn fool had given him only home telephone numbers.

Yet that might be just as well. One couldn't be too careful in a case involving national security. The tentacles ran deep on this caper – even O'Brien, of all people, was under suspicion – and office telephones had been tapped before.

Hardison considered for a moment and then made up his mind. Actually, the information he had was too important to be passed on the telephone, be it at home or office. It ought to be given personally.

The sergeant collected his pipe and tobacco and struggled into his coat. He'd be sitting on the doorstep when Shaver showed up, he thought, and it would be the right doorstep, too. The lady friend's.

He went out telling himself that you couldn't fool an old harness bull.

Shaver sat smoking while the bank manager toyed nervously with the name plate that identified him as F. Mortimer Delphe. It was him, not the manager, who ought to be nervous, Shaver reflected. Forging a court order was a very serious offense, and it hadn't been that good a forgery, either.

'I can't imagine what's taking so long,' Delphe said, discarding the name plate in favor of his ink stand. 'It's really quite a simple matter. Unless there's more than one account.'

'I doubt it,' Shaver said. He puffed carefully on his cigarette and wondered where the ashtray had disappeared to. It had been right in front of him a minute ago. The manager kept rearranging everything. 'But one never knows, does one?'

Delphe nodded solemnly. He was newly appointed to his position and was convinced that much more was afoot than what the court order implied. The Mounties didn't come nosing around without good reason. This could lead to God knows what.

There was a knock on the door and the owlish accountant who had been assigned the search entered with a pretty young teller in tow. 'Sorry,' he said breathlessly, passing a folder to Delphe. 'I had to chase all over.' He glanced at the girl. 'Mary will explain. She handled it.'

Delphe coughed discreetly. 'Mr. Shaver here is a police officer.'

'Mr. Crichton warned me,' the girl said, smiling at Shaver. 'Mr. Bjsgrkowski came in this morning. Just before noon . . .' The smile blinked off when she saw the look on his face. 'Is something wrong?'

'No,' Shaver lied. 'It's just a pain that strikes me now and again. I was badly beaten once by a karate expert.' He searched deep inside for the necessary strength to continue. 'What you're going to tell me is that he suddenly closed his account without explanation?'

'Why, yes,' she said, the smile returning. 'Both of them.'

Shaver thought that a karate beating was something a girl could accept cheerfully. It wasn't like chronic post-nasal drip or terminal hemorrhoids. He swung back to Delphe. 'I take it those are they?'

The manager mumbled unintelligibly. He had the folder open and was searching vainly for the awful truth. Accounts pilfered. Bank bilked.

'After you,' Shaver said. There was no rush now. Bjsgrkowski was long gone. He had started covering his spoor as soon as he got word of the foul-up at Riverview.

'Is that all?' the girl wanted to know.

'No,' Shaver told her. 'I'll probably have a few questions. Once Mr. Delphe . . .' He finally located the ashtray tucked in the out basket. 'Think of how you'd describe him for one of those wanted posters they put up in the Post Office.'

The manager swallowed hard and surrendered the folder. Shaver smiled his thanks and lifted the cover and couldn't help but whistle softly.

'What's wrong . . . ?'

'Nothing,' Shaver said, getting out his notebook. 'I'm just surprised by the size of the initial deposit.'

'It's not unusual,' Delphe said defensively. 'Businessmen often need a large supply of ready cash. We've had current accounts running into several millions of dollars.'

'No doubt,' Shaver admitted, busy copying dates and figures. 'But I'm impressed all the same.'

Bjsgrkowski's current account had been opened the previous July with a cash deposit of $500,000. In the ensuing two months, there had been large and frequent withdrawals, ranging up to $49,999.99, and the balance had stood just short of $6,000 at the end of September. The account had then remained dormant until the purchase of the Rover.

'What's the significance of keeping his checks below $50,000?' Shaver asked.

'It's the cut-off point,' the owlish accountant volunteered. 'We keep a microfilm record of any current account transaction over $50,000. If it's less than that, the canceled checks are simply returned to the depositor, and he's responsible for his own records.'

'So, except for this last transaction, the only one recorded since September, you have no knowledge of to whom any of the other payments were made? The canceled checks have all gone back to Bjsgrkowski at his postal box address?'

'That's correct.'

Shaver examined the personal checking account and decided that it simply provided a living allowance. It had been opened on the same date as the current account with a deposit of $10,000. There had been frequent cash withdrawals averaging about $2,000 monthly. The balance on closing was $800.

'Well,' Shaver said, closing the folder. 'So much for his sex life. Now what about a description of the gentleman?'

'Gee,' the girl said. 'I've been thinking about that. I don't know if I can be of much help.' Her shoulders hunched up desperately. 'He was so darn plain-looking.'

Shaver nodded morosely. He thought that a few other things were also plain enough. Bjsgrkowski was the 'money man' for an elaborate criminal operation. He had paid out almost half a million dollars in preparation for the big event. The Rover had been the last major purchase necessary to the plan and zero hour was rapidly approaching.

Ten

It would have been much simpler to tear off the pertinent part, but Sub-Inspector Benson's mind didn't work that way, so he submitted all the evidence – the whole roll of teletype copy – to Inspector McDermott.

'It struck me as kind of strange when I saw it,' Benson reported, lowering himself into a chair. 'You couldn't have requested the thing. You were tied up all day Monday with Regina versus Kemelman.'

McDermott frowned in answer – what was the old woman onto now? – and the furrows in his brow only deepened when he read the exchange of messages with the computer at Central Data. Henke? Who in the hell was Henke?

'I thought I should draw it to your attention,' Benson said.

'You thought right,' McDermott admitted. He read Henke's brief file summary once more and didn't like any of it. He didn't like it at all.

'I made a few preliminary inquiries,' Benson said. 'No one will own up in Communications. So it must be the D cups from Records.'

'Kirchoff?'

'Who else?'

Several sets of mammary glands bounced before McDermott's eyes before he grasped the meaning of Benson's question. Kirchoff, he remembered, was the only one from Records who was allowed in the Communications Room, so the bra size really wasn't pertinent. He wished that Benson didn't have the habit of wandering all over the place like a demented cow.

'I can't see any other possibility,' Benson said, pressing his case. 'If an officer wanted a secret file, he'd simply use his own name, and no one would think twice. It's only some-body without their own authorization who'd pull this kind of stunt.'

'Right again,' McDermott said, becoming annoyed. He wished that Benson would learn to leave well enough alone. The man had done a good job and now he was spoiling it. There was no need to demonstrate his marvelous grasp of the obvious.

'Shall I call her in?' Benson asked.

'I think not,' McDermott decided. 'We could be onto something big here. It might be wise to probe deeper before the confrontation.'

Benson thought that he had detected a mild reprieve. It perhaps was time to withdraw. 'I'll leave it to you, then ...'

'Why don't you do that?' McDermott agreed, turning back to the teletype copy. He thought that this should teach Benson once and for all. The loudmouth had talked himself right off a case.

Benson had been gone for several minutes before all the implications sank in and McDermott realized that he had been duped. A bad apple in the office ... security not up to snuff ... a foreign government in the act ...

Goddam, McDermott thought. This could get awfully sticky before all the facts were in. No one in his right mind would want the thing. So what was he doing with it?

Shaver left the bank and walked over to the Georgia Pub. He told himself that this was where he mustered out. Something very big indeed was brewing and he was powerless to halt it on his own. Half a million dollars could finance an army, and one against an army was lousy odds.

He ordered two draft beers and sat nursing them despondently. The only proper course, he knew, was to confess his duplicity, so that the real cloak-and-dagger types at Special Branch could step in and save the day. It meant being drummed out of the force in disgrace, but that was much the lesser evil awaiting him.

If he persisted in going it alone? If he gambled for a miracle and lost? If Kosygin was killed as a result of his deception ...?

Well, he wouldn't have to worry about a discharge then, Shaver thought. The kindest thing they'd do is hang him. And not necessarily by the neck.

Shaver finished his beer – there's nothing like a couple of drinks to prompt some sober thinking – and admitted one other compelling reason for screaming for help. The plotters were hot on the trail of his own sweet arse. He could get himself killed playing lone wolf.

Confess, you blighter, Shaver thought, and he dug out a dime and went to the pay phone in the lobby and called Petapiece at The Stump Club.

'Black John?' the bartender said. 'No, he's not here, goddam it, and don't call again. This ain't no dating service . . .'

'Could you tell me when he left?' Shaver asked, surprised at the bartender's vicious mood. He normally was pleasant enough.

'Hours ago,' the bartender said, slamming down the phone.

Shaver hung up wondering what Petapiece was trying to pull. He claimed to spend the day at the club and twice now the opposite was true. It was a slipshod way for a control to act. Supposing something important came up?

Supposing? You are daft, Shaver thought. He hesitated only a moment and then got out another dime and dialed RCMP Vancouver Sub-division. It didn't matter whom he told. Just as long as it was someone in authority. And what better bastard to burden than his great and good friend McDermott?

Shelagh, the inspector's secretary, fairly gushed at the sound of his voice. 'Tim? It's about time. We were thinking you dead. Not so much as a peep in weeks . . .' She caught herself and assumed a more businesslike tone. 'I imagine it's the old man you're wanting?'

'Yes,' Shaver admitted.

'Well,' Shelagh said. 'That's tough. You'll have to settle for me. He went out of here a good half hour ago.'

'For the day?'

'Not to return.'

'It's barely four-thirty,' Shaver complained. 'He never leaves before six. Did he say where he was headed?'

'No,' Shelagh said. 'He's to call in when he's settled.' There was a pause while she considered alternatives. 'Benson is around somewhere. Does that help?'

Shaver grimaced. Benson was an old lady. He'd swoon if this rat was tossed in his lap. There was no choice but to go to the top. 'I think not. Would you mind switching me to the assistant commissioner's office?'

'If you want. But I'm warning you. He's away playing golf somewhere.'

'You mean Benson's senior in charge?'

'I do.'

'Good-by,' Shaver said, not wishing to be tempted. 'When McDermott checks in, tell him I was calling, and ask him to sit still for a while. I've got something important and I'll be back to you for his number within the hour. Okay?'

'Sure.'

Shaver hung up and returned to his table for a couple more beers and decided that a celebration was in order. It wasn't every day that you chucked a lifetime's work and it was only once that you turned in the scarlet.

He left the pub and walked over to Inglis Reid, the Town's best butcher shop, bar none, and spent a fortune on two porterhouse steaks. To be listed on his expense account as a bribe, he thought. Bogna was a meat eater. Her nostrils flared when the blood sizzled. You had to serve her quick or she'd drown in her own saliva. Then he went around the corner to the specialty liquor store and bought a bottle of Something Special. Bogna would relish a shot or two, but it was mostly for him, he admitted, and damn the cost. He wasn't going out with cheap booze on his breath.

By the time his taxi arrived at Bogna's apartment, Shaver was almost pleased with his situation, thinking that it took a terrible wrench such as this to set a man on his proper course in life. The Mounties really weren't for him. Fifteen years and still a corporal. Some career.

He tipped the cabbie fifty cents, twice as much as his custom, and went whistling into the building, visions of greener fields dancing in his head. He saw a frosted glass door with his name lettered on it and something suitably dashing below. CONFIDENTIAL INVESTIGATIONS.

The image faded and was replaced by the reality of Bogna's locked door. He knocked twice and got no answer. Nor was there any response when he called.

Shaver frowned. It wasn't like her to be this late getting home. Had she come and gone? He went back to the stairs, the third one down and got the key from under the runner. He kept wondering what in the hell was going on.

There was nothing in the flat to tell him. He wasted five minutes' drinking time searching for a message and then gave up and broke open the scotch. He looked around for a proper glory cup – this, after all, was a celebration – and spotted the silver mug he'd been awarded as barracks shuffleboard champ. He put the bottle aside and crossed the living room and took the mug from the fireplace mantel.

What was this? The hollowed-out base of the mug had a folded envelope wadded up inside. Shaver pulled it out and saw that it was official stationery. His mind leaped. Henke's file?

Shaver tore open the envelope and removed a single sheet of paper and then froze at the sound of the door creaking behind him.

Goliath let go of the fire-escape ladder and dropped heavily to the ground. He hunched there a moment, getting his breath back, waiting for his heart to stop pounding. The colonel would be furious, he thought. Frothing at the mouth. Blind with rage.

A car came into the parking lot at the rear of the building and stopped only a few feet away from him. The woman driver got out and stared at him curiously.

'Is there anything wrong?' the woman asked.

'No,' Goliath told her. 'It's nothing. I just tripped and fell.'

The woman heard the creaking noise above her head and glanced up to see the fire-escape ladder still swinging back and forth. When she looked back her eyes couldn't hide the knowledge that would soon cost her so dearly.

'Don't,' Goliath said softly.

The woman opened her mouth and Goliath sprang from his crouch like some jungle cat pouncing on its prey. He closed his hand around her throat and snuffed out both her scream and her life in the same instant.

Almost in the same motion, Goliath had the car door open, the woman's body stuffed down on the floor on the passenger's side, his own huge frame hunched behind the wheel. He dumped the woman's purse out on the seat and got her keys and started the car. He backed out of the lot and drove away.

One, two, what did it matter? Goliath thought, glancing at the woman's crumpled body. The colonel would be furious.

'Well,' McDermott said. 'Fancy meeting you here.' He stood at the threshold a long moment, and although he did his best to hide it, he obviously was very surprised. 'I didn't know.'

'Know what?' Shaver said stupidly, equally rattled by the inspector's sudden appearance in the doorway. It wasn't just that they hadn't spoken since Shaver had poked him and McDermott had laid the disciplinary charge. McDermott was positively the last man who should come barging into Bogna's flat. The inspector had worked hard for his station and he liked to keep it. This wasn't his side of town.

'That you got your mail here, for one thing,' McDermott said. He was on the verge of leaving, but then changed his mind, pulling his scarf from around his neck in a deliberate, familiar way. 'How long have you two . . . ?' Once more he checked himself. 'I'm sorry. That's hardly my business, is it?'

'A couple of years,' Shaver said, prepared to calculate the months, days and hours if requested. McDermott had a perfect right to know that he was diddling someone from the office, and how long it had been going on, and what positions were preferred. What was strange about the question was that he should have to ask it. An inspector ought to have his men checked on better.

'That long?' McDermott said, smiling faintly. He stepped inside and closed the door behind him and looked the flat over. He stuffed his scarf into an already crowded pocket, one end of it dangling a foot, as usual, and began the slow process of unbuttoning his overcoat. 'You had me fooled, I must say. I never thought to connect you two.' He reflected on how he might rationalize this oversight. 'She's a bit on the mature side, isn't she?'

'There's mileage left,' Shaver said. Ordinarily, he might have put up a better defense, but his mind was on the sheet of paper, still unfolded and unread, stuck in his hand like a hot stone. If it was Henke's file – and what else could it be? – this could spell disaster for Bogna. Her security clearance didn't give her the right to request secret files without proper authorization – and it especially didn't permit her to bring them home.

'If you say so,' McDermott decided, again smiling faintly. He looked at the sheet of paper. 'What's wrong? Afraid of bad news?'

'Junk mail,' Shaver told him, and he felt certain McDermott knew the truth, or at the very least suspected. That would explain the surprise visit. 'It'll keep . . .' Shaver fought the impulse to stuff the thing in his pocket – that would really look suspicious – and instead tossed it carelessly on a lamp table. 'Could you manage a drink?'

McDermott seemed distracted readily enough. He glanced appreciatively at the bottle of Something Special. 'If that's what you're serving.'

'It is,' Shaver said. He took the inspector's coat and steered him over to the sofa and made a point of waiting until he sat down. 'How do you like it?'

'Neat,' McDermott said. He settled back and got out his cigarettes and lit up. 'That's to ensure I get a fair portion. I'm not unaware of your reputation.'

Shaver flushed slightly but said nothing. It was remarks like that which had finally proved his undoing with McDermott. One joke too many about Shaver pinching pennies till the Queen got a nosebleed.

'Will she be long?' McDermott called after him.

'I shouldn't think so,' Shaver said. He got the glasses from the cupboard and wondered how he could destroy Henke's file without McDermott noticing. Before he confessed his sins, he had to get rid of that incriminating sheet of paper. It wouldn't do to drag Bogna down into the muck with him.

McDermott didn't answer and Shaver quickly poured

two stiff drinks and returned to the living room. He told himself that the fireplace was the answer. He'd light the gas and then casually pick up the supposed piece of junk mail ...

'Thanks,' McDermott murmured, taking his glass. He leaned forward and raised it in a sort of half-hearted toast. He had intended to wait for a better time but decided it was now or never. 'No hard feelings?'

Shaver didn't know what to say.

'I've been meaning to tell you,' McDermott said, looking a bit ruddier than usual. 'That haymaker you tossed at me. I guess I deserved it.'

Shaver stood staring down at him unsurely. His mind refused to function.

'There's got to be the hearing, of course,' McDermott said. 'It's too late to stop that. But you've my word it'll only be a formality. I'll admit my provocation and the most you'll get is a slap on the wrist.' He resorted to bluster to cover his embarrassment. 'That's sufficient, isn't it, damn you? Do you need an apology besides a month's vacation?'

Shaver still couldn't find any words to answer. How could McDermott peddle a story exactly opposite to that handed him by Petapiece? How could McDermott not know that he was working undercover for Special Branch?

It didn't make sense, Shaver thought. Petapiece had talked to McDermott before giving him the assignment. McDermott had recommended him for the job. Shaver could plainly recall Petapiece's exact words. *McDermott may hate your guts – but he speaks highly of your resourcefulness.*

'Well, bugger you, then,' McDermott said harshly. He slammed his drink down and pushed to his feet. 'You'll get no apology from me.'

Shaver was lost in another world. Mad questions kept exploding inside his head. Supposing Petapiece is the worst kind of liar? Supposing the grubby little mooch isn't with Special Branch at all? Supposing, corporal, that he's played you for the fool that you are, and supposing his motive – is what?

McDermott blundered about the room looking for his coat. He finally found it and was about to leave when he saw the folded sheet of paper on the lamp table. It struck him that the faint blue lines on the back were awfully familiar. The mark of the special type of paper used in the copier at the sub-division.

It's what you came after in the first place, he told himself, picking it up. His anger subsided and a pleasant warmth enveloped him. Inspector McDermott triumphs again. The mystery solved in jig time. And Shaver's balls as a bonus.

'Hey,' Shaver said, finally finding his voice. 'That's private.'

'Junk mail, eh?' McDermott said. He turned as he unfolded the paper. 'A nice try. But it didn't work.'

Shaver stood watching helplessly. He wished the fates would arrive at a decision and stick to it. He had slipped the noose but a second ago. Now the rope was settling around his neck again.

'They shot it?' McDermott said. His expression slowly changed – he was a punctured inner tube withering away – and it seemed to take all his remaining strength to crumple the paper and toss it on the floor. Then he pushed past Shaver wordlessly and slammed out of the flat.

Shaver finished his own drink and what remained of McDermott's before retrieving the paper. He smoothed it open prepared for anything. There was just the one brief paragraph: 'Did you hear about the two Polacks who went hunting and followed some tracks for miles and miles? Finally they spotted a train – and shot it.'

This wasn't possible, Shaver thought. He had stuffed the joke in the mug himself – how long ago? It had been ages. Well over a year. He had stopped hiding the damn things for Bogna to find after she had bopped him with the frying pan. And what had made her so bloody mad? A swimming pool full of Polack girls – Bay of Pigs.

Shaver crumpled the paper once more and took it to the bathroom. He found something jammed against the door and when he finally pushed inside he discovered that this annoying deadweight was the corpse of Detective Sergeant Hardison. Hardison had used a piece of soap to scrawl a message on the tile floor before he succumbed to the stiletto in the small of his back.

'HENKE AM,' the message in the soap said.

Shaver shook his head. Hardison's grammar had always been atrocious. It should be Henke *is*, not am, for God's sake, and it was shitty of him not to finish the message.

Is what?

Eleven

Bogna entered her flat and found Shaver waiting. Her anger flared anew and she berated herself for not coming straight home from work. If she had grabbed the extra key from its hiding place, she could have kept the bastard locked out, she thought. Kicking him out would be more difficult. But he was going all the same.

'I thought you got the message,' Bogna said stiffly.

Shaver was staring into his glass of scotch. He didn't bother looking at her. 'Which one?'

'The one about you not being welcome here any more.'

'That one,' Shaver said, still not looking at her. 'Don't worry. I'll be going soon enough.' He pushed slowly to his feet. 'I'm only here to catch you when you faint. There's a corpse in your can.'

'How very amusing.'

'See for yourself.'

There was something in his tone that made her look and she would have screamed had he not followed behind and clamped a huge hand over her mouth.

'Easy,' Shaver whispered. 'Easy. Easy . . .' He turned her around with her mouth still muffled. 'I don't want the neighbors to know. Understand?'

She nodded and he removed his hand and she leaned back against the wall for support. It was a long time before she could speak. 'Did you . . . ?'

'No,' Shaver said softly. 'I didn't.' He thought it strange that she should ask such a question. If she suspected at all that this was his work, you'd think she'd be halfway down the stairs by now, yelling bloody murder. 'I just found it occupied when I went to pee.'

'Who . . . ?'

'Detective Sergeant Hardison,' Shaver said. 'Late of the

city homicide squad. He was doing a little snooping on my behalf and it seems he hit pay dirt. I figure he came here to tell me the good news and somebody was laying in wait.'

'Waiting *here?*'

'For me, not him,' Shaver said. 'There's some killers want me dead and they're watching all my hangouts. Posted at every bar in town, and half the whorehouses, too. I doubt I'll survive the night.'

'This isn't funny.'

'I'm glad you agree,' Shaver said. 'I was hoping you might see it my way.' He poured her a stiff drink of the scotch and stood watching while she tossed it down. 'I need your help if I'm to stay alive. What's your answer?'

Her eyes met his and a little flash of anger showed. 'You have to ask?'

'I guess not,' Shaver told her, looking away. 'And thanks ...' He poured her another glass of scotch and one for himself and went back into the living room. He motioned her to the sofa and sat down in a chair and got out his Sweet Caps. 'You ready?'

'Yes.'

'Okay,' Shaver said. 'It goes this way: You left work and went downtown and had dinner and took in a movie. You had coffee somewhere afterward and you didn't get home until around midnight and that's when you found the stiff. You called the police and you didn't tell them anything when they came because you didn't know anything. It was a complete and utter mystery to you how the strange gentleman came to expire in your boudoir. Got that?'

'Yes.'

'Good,' Shaver said. 'There's just a couple three other things. If for any reason this business gets too difficult for you, just clam up, completely and absolutely, until noon tomorrow. If you haven't heard from me by then, tell the police everything you know, not leaving out a word, and make especially sure they get my last will and testament. It's hidden in one of your Books of Knowledge. Under F for Fables. Got that?'

'Yes.'

'Good,' Shaver repeated. 'And now for my last request. May I *please* see that F-I-L-E?'

Bogna nodded and got up and crossed to the fireplace. She took a pottery piggy bank from the mantel and broke it open against the brick facing. She picked a piece of folded paper from the litter that had fallen to the floor and delivered it to Shaver.

'I'm sorry,' she said. 'I thought this was pretty hilarious when I first read it. I guess I was wrong.'

Shaver unfolded it and saw that Hardison's grammar wasn't so bad after all. HENKE AM meant Henke American.

The information from the computer read as follows:

HENKE, RUDOLPH IVOR, BORN 6 AUG 1925, DOR, LATVIA. UNMARRIED. NO KNOWN NEXT OF KIN. FAMILY ALLEGEDLY SLAUGHTERED BY RUSSIAN TROOPS WORLD WAR II. POST-WAR REFUGEE IMMIGRANT TO UNITED STATES. ENTERED CANADA AS LANDED IMMIGRANT MAR 1962. OBTAINED CITIZENSHIP DEC 1968. SUSPECTED SEX DEVIATE. SEVERAL ARRESTS AND CONVICTIONS FOR OBSTRUCTING POLICE AND PROPERTY DAMAGE IN VARIOUS PROTEST DEMONSTRATIONS. EMPLOYED MINOR CAPACITY BY U.S. CENTRAL INTELLIGENCE AGENCY. CURRENT ASSIGNMENT CHECKING ON U.S. NATIONALS IN RADICAL GROUPS IN BRITISH COLUMBIA.

Oh, it was funny enough, Shaver thought. The CIA certainly didn't want any harm to befall Kosygin, and even if it did, it wouldn't assign someone of Henke's ilk to do the job. So you could have a good laugh at the KGB. Imagine them being so stupid as to put some CIA puke at the top of their surveillance list for Kosygin's visit to Canada? And you could also have a good laugh at Corporal Shaver. His supposedly important assignment was mere window dressing. Its only purpose was to satisfy the stupid Nervous Nellies in the KGB.

Quite a spectacle, all in all, and there was a time when he might have managed a couple of giggles himself, Shaver thought. But not any more. The joke had backfired somewhere along the line. The CIA puke had disappeared and a perfumed killer was floating in the Fraser and a sergeant of the police was dead beside the toilet bowl.

'Does this change your plans?' Bogna asked.

Shaver finally got around to laughing. 'What plans?'

The colonel methodically worked his way around the office. He used only his stump, slashing wildly, and this tended to minimize the destruction, but it was still formidable to behold. What couldn't be broken was knocked over. Pictures went sailing off the walls. Whole shelves of books were dumped en masse.

Samuel stood watching fearfully. The destruction as such didn't bother him. His records were safe and they were all that mattered. Nor was he concerned about the noise. The other tenants in the building had left and the janitor wouldn't be around for hours.

What worried him was the time being wasted by this childish temper tantrum. Time was so very, very important. They needed every minute of it. So much had gone wrong and needed correction. Unless they started soon, they'd never get it done, and if they didn't do it, the operation would surely fail. And if they failed . . . ?

Samuel shuddered involuntarily. He didn't like to think about what would happen if the operation was a failure. He shut that out of his mind and tried to concentrate on recommendations. The maniac who unfortunately functioned as his superior would want recommendations when this was over. That was one good thing to be said for these tantrums. They left him spent and open to suggestion.

The first recommendation, of course, would be to kill Shaver, not try to take him alive. The slippery weasel was far, far too dangerous to let live any longer, and the operation could succeed without him. It meant a drastic revision of plans but it nevertheless could be done. The intended results could be achieved by using just Petapiece.

When he was near the point of collapse, the colonel fell gasping into a chair, his face the color of an overripe cherry, his stump battered and bleeding. Samuel got himself ready. He'd be asked his opinion soon – and his first recommendation would be to have Goliath commit another murder.

Shaver left Bogna's flat thinking that his luck might have

changed at last. He was going to have a long heart-to-heart chat with Petapiece. If it turned out that Petapiece wasn't with Special Branch — if the grubby mooch was trying to pull a fast one for some as yet unfathomable reason — then there was a light shining at the end of the tunnel. It meant that he didn't have to confess his duplicity and be drummed out of the force.

Why should he confess? With Hardison dead, there were only two other persons, Petapiece and Bogna, who could connect him to Henke. Bogna would never tell on him in a thousand years. So that left only Petapiece posing a threat.

The way things stood, there was a good chance for a saw-off, Shaver thought. Petapiece would be anxious to make a deal when he realized he had been found out. He'd keep his mouth shut in exchange for a running start — and when he was out of the picture the rest would be roses.

Shaver didn't have it worked out to the last detail — he'd have to fill those in as he went along — but he had the over-all grand design firmly fixed in his mind: It wasn't Petapiece who had put him onto Henke. He had somehow managed that part all by himself. There had been a reason, a good reason, why he was interested in Henke, and why he should discuss Henke's disappearance with Detective Sergeant Hardison. Then, because of this contact, an attempt was made on his life, leading him to stumble upon an apparent plot to assassinate Kosygin.

Simple?

Yes, Shaver decided, and if he could sell that story to McDermott, he'd be a hero, not a dupe. He could save his own life as well as Kosygin's. He could get a medal instead of being booted out on his arse.

It was a wonderful dream and Shaver was determined to make it come true. All it required was that Petapiece be a phony and that he be willing to co-operate. Please, please, make him a phony, Shaver prayed. He told himself this was the only thing necessary. Petapiece would co-operate. He'd co-operate — or else.

Inspector McDermott telephoned his office and asked

Shelagh what was new and she told him about the message left by Shaver. Both made small mistakes, Shelagh in not mentioning the time Shaver had telephoned her, and McDermott in thinking that Shaver was trying to patch up their latest set-to at Bogna's flat.

'Is that all?' McDermott asked, thinking that Shaver could go to hell.

'Yes.'

'Well,' McDermott said, 'if he calls again before you leave, tell him you didn't hear from me, and make sure the night switchboard gets the same message. Inspector McDermott is unavailable to Corporal Shaver.'

'All right,' Shelagh said doubtfully.

'I'm at the Terminal City Club,' McDermott said. 'Home around ten. To bed by midnight. No calls after that – except to announce the end of the world.'

'All right.'

'And cheer up,' McDermott ordered, hanging up. He wondered what the ladies saw in a long drink of water like Shaver. By the looks of it, Shaver was practically living with the D cups from Records, and by the sounds of it, he had Shelagh mooning over him, too.

One more puzzle to ponder, McDermott thought. He went to the bar and ordered a drink and stood brooding over their encounter at Bogna's flat. He'd made such a bloody fool of himself with that stupid Polish joke, and it was all Benson's fault, too. The old woman was probably off a mile. In all likelihood, it was one of the communications clerks, not the D cups from Records, who had pulled that stunt with Henke's file. Their denying the fact didn't make them innocent. Besides, with Shaver involved, that cleared the D cups, didn't it? Any woman stupid enough to get mixed up with him hardly qualified as a Mata Hari.

McDermott caught himself and had to admit that this was woolly thinking. It was Shaver who figured as the prime suspect. On suspension a month and drinking Something Special. It wasn't natural for a tightwad to toss money around during lean times. That was goddam suspicious . . .

Across the room, a billiard cue was raised in challenge, to which McDermott smilingly responded. Even police inspectors needed their diversions, he decided. If Shaver actually was involved, it must be very minor league stuff indeed, and it would certainly keep until morning.

That was McDermott's Rule: Never run to a fire. If it's a good one, it'll still be burning when you get there.

Shaver sat at The Stump Club bar watching the one-handed dart player who fancied himself another Yul Brynner. For a chap who spent so much time at the game, he wasn't much of a marksman, Shaver thought. A child could beat him blindfolded.

'Where's Black John these days?' Shaver asked casually, his back to the bartender. 'I haven't seen him for a while.'

'Dead, for all I know,' the bartender said. He took his rag and hobbled to the other end of the bar. He was bloody bored with the subject of Black John.

'You think he's sick?' Shaver asked, turning around.

'For all I care,' the bartender said.

Shaver got out his Sweet Caps. The fates conspiring again, he thought. It had been a polite inquiry and it had deserved a civil answer. Why now of all times should the bartender be sullen and unco-operative? 'I was only asking . . .'

'And you got your answer,' the bartender said. He'd recently had the police in about Black John. They had listened patiently to his suspicions – and then gone away laughing.

Jesus, Shaver thought. He lit his cigarette and inhaled deeply and held the smoke for as long as he could. When this was over, he'd go away somewhere, he decided. Someplace where it was warm and sunny and everybody was happy and friendly and the girls screwed for quarters and the bartenders were always smiling.

'We've been pretty chummy,' Shaver said, the smoke blowing out in a seemingly endless stream. 'I'd like to visit the bloke if he's sick. You wouldn't happen to know his address?'

'I know it.'

'Well . . . ?'

'How come you have to ask?' the bartender said. 'That strikes me as odd. Especially since you're so goddam chummy.'

Shaver took another deep drag on his cigarette. He told himself he'd stay at the very best hotel and eat at the finest restaurants and visit all the top entertainment spots. A chap could have a lot of fun in this great big wonderful world. The secret was to just let yourself go – and to scrupulously avoid shitheads.

'How did you lose your leg?' Shaver asked.

The bartender paused in his work. He put the rag aside so both hands would be free. 'I donated it to science . . .'

'Your balls, too?' Shaver asked. 'Or did they just wither and fall off? Rotted from lack of use?'

'I say,' the dart player protested. 'Why start a war over an address?' He positioned himself so that he was between the bartender and Shaver. 'Black John lives in Gastown. Number 8 Maple Tree Square.'

Shaver wondered how he had snuck up so quietly. 'Thanks . . .'

'My pleasure,' the dart player said, smiling. 'I'm not very fond of wars.' He lifted his battered stump for Shaver's examination. 'It's how I lost the thing.'

'I'm sorry.'

'No need to be sorry,' the dart player said. 'It taught me a valuable lesson. Never lend your hand to the devil's work. You may not get it back.'

How true, Shaver thought. He showed the bartender a finger and departed the premises.

Petapiece smiled contentedly and pushed away the last platter. No man could ask for more, he decided. Steamed crab. Pan-fried prawns with garlic and black beans. Deep-fried whole rock cod in a sweet-and-sour sauce. A banquet that would grace a royal table and no king would have found greater pleasure in it.

He lit a cigarette and sat smoking and drinking the last of his tea while the Chinese waiter cleared the table. He thought that it wasn't such a bad world after all and that he did all right by himself and that he shouldn't let the bum boys upstairs get under his skin. They were a sad lot, playing politics the whole day through, not knowing who to trust nor depend on, and they were more to be pitied than anything else.

They'd never get him in no office, Petapiece thought. It was too goddam dangerous there. You never knew who was going to stick a knife in your back. Down in the trenches, you at least had a fair-to-middling idea of who was the enemy, and you generally knew from which direction they'd be attacking.

The waiter returned with his bill and Petapiece gave the boy an extra two dollars and waved him away. This was his night to raise a bit of hell and he was going to do it properly. There was no telling where he might end up before the evening was over. Perhaps dancing at the Panorama Roof.

Petapiece smiled – how long had it been since he last tripped the light fantastic? – and dropped his cigarette in his teacup. He thought that it wouldn't do to step out of character to quite that extent. Black John's idea of raising hell required a bottle of wine and a whore. He'd find a ready supply of both on the short walk home from Chinatown.

Shaver showed his badge to the big barrel of a woman known to her tenants as Mother Mac. 'I'm looking for a man who's supposed to live here,' he told her. 'There's a one-word description been put out on him. He's dirty.'

'Black John?' Mother Mac said.

'That's him,' Shaver admitted.

Mother Mac took another hard look at the badge and satisfied herself as to its authenticity. 'He's not home . . .'

'Nor should you expect him,' Shaver said. 'If he knows what's good, he's halfway to China by now, destination Outer Mongolia. We can't extradite from there.'

'He's run off?'

'He has.'

'Oh shit,' Mother Mac said, her face draining white. The scrawny runt owed her two weeks' back rent. *Two weeks!*'

'You mind showing his room?' Shaver asked. 'I'd like to poke around if it's okay with you. There might be some hint as to where he's headed.'

Mother Mac nodded dully and went to get the key. She

wanted to poke around herself. It was highly unlikely, but if the room held anything of true value, she had first claim. 'This way . . .'

Shaver gave her a good head start – that elephant's rump would crush him if she slipped – and then went up the stairs convinced that Petapiece was a phony. It was one thing for a control to sit around in a dingy club all day for the sake of a good cover. But to come home to this dump in the bargain? Not flipping likely.

It was much more probable that Petapiece had been hired by the plotters to play the role of a control for Special Branch. What their exact motive was, Shaver still couldn't guess, but they no doubt had good reason for such a crazy ploy, he thought. It was somehow essential to their plot that an idiot Mountie and a CIA puke become entangled in the web.

'What's he done?' Mother Mac asked, breathing heavily.

'Sex crimes most foul,' Shaver decided. 'Small children. Animals . . .' He wondered if he was carrying things too far and concluded it wasn't half far enough. 'The man's a fiend. There's been nothing like his bestiality since the Dark Ages.'

Mother Mac stopped and turned. She had a slightly glazed look and her jaw hung open.

'Why God permits such a monster to exist,' Shaver lamented. 'They'll have to clear the public gallery if he's ever brought to trial. Those that didn't swoon at the evidence would climb over the rail and tear him apart with their bare hands.'

'Black John . . . ?'

'The name fits,' Shaver said. 'It'll take its doubtful place in history. Jack the Ripper. The Marquis de Sade . . .' He caught the key as it fell and slipped around her as she leaned against the wall. 'Incidentally, you didn't ever see him bring in frogs, did you? He's done the strangest things ever to frogs.'

Mother Mac didn't answer – she was wondering if she could make it back downstairs before she got sick – and Shaver went up the last flight alone and let himself into

Petapiece's flat. He thought he might have overdone it a little. He didn't want the grubby mooch killed. Or at least not yet.

Petapiece backed out of the building thinking that had been an awfully close call. He shoved the bottle of wine at the whore and told her to take it and leave. When she started to protest, he took ten dollars from his wallet, held it up for her to see, and then pressed it into her hand.

The whore was still inclined to protest – she was cold and it was a long walk to her room – but the wild look in Peta-piece's eyes changed her mind. She drew herself up and shrugged her shoulders indifferently. She decided that he was too dirty for her tastes anyway.

Petapiece pushed past her and hurried down the street. His stride increased with each step and soon he was running. He disappeared around the corner just as a black Chrysler pulled to the curb on the other side of Maple Tree Square.

Shaver couldn't make up his mind. Petapiece's flat was as much a puzzle as the man himself. The top floor of a flop-house – a couple of crummy rooms in a battered tenement on skid road – and yet the place was clean, goddam it, clean! The dishes were washed and the floor had been swept. There was new linen on the bed and the toilet didn't need flushing.

Which means? Shaver asked himself, staring and wonder-ing. He had to admit jumping to conclusions coming up the stairs. Once you got in the door, this wasn't that bad a place to hang your hat, all things considered. There were pictures on the wall and plants on the window sill. There were good books to read and radio if you'd rather listen and even tele-vision if all else failed.

So what if the neighbors weren't exactly socialites? You could just as easy find a drunken sot next door if you lived in Shaughnessy. A chap who kept his door locked and minded his manners and used tunnel vision when necessary might actually enjoy residing in Gastown.

Shaver crossed to the window and stared down at the statue of Gassy Jack Deighton in Maple Tree Square. It all depended on your point of view, he thought. He'd been trained as a cop and he saw things with a cop's eyes. The kids spinny on drugs and the rubbies crawling drunk and the Indian whores old women at twenty.

The tourists obviously saw something else. The historic buildings and the colorful cafes. The street vendors and the antique stores. The bargain basements and the specialty shops. The crummy stuff they hardly noticed and just shrugged off if they did. It was not going to spoil their day.

And Petapiece?

Well, if he was what he claimed to be, he saw a damn good place to hide, Shaver thought. He swore and got out his Sweet Caps. The sad truth was that the flat didn't prove anything one way or another and he'd been a fool to think it might. What in the hell had he been afraid of finding? A secret radio transmitter? Code books? False mustaches? Did the absence of cloak-and-dagger trappings prove his theory that Petapiece was a fake?

Shaver smiled at his idiocy and was about to light his cigarette when he thought he saw the statue move. Oh, come now, he told himself. You've been drinking *good* scotch. Statues don't . . .

The figure of a giant – an incredibly huge ox of a man – stepped out of the shadows next to the statue and slipped into a darkened doorway. Shaver remembered with a start that he had seen such a man that morning at Riverview. Examining the innards of a supposedly stalled Chrysler.

Now he was back, and those other men moving furtively in the street below were his companions.

Shaver edged away from the window. He had expected the bastards to pick up his trail sooner or later. They wanted him dead and there was no good reason why they should stop trying. Yet he had hoped to keep one step ahead until he'd had his chat with Petapiece.

Some other time, Shaver thought grimly, unholstering his Webley. It looked as though they were closing in on the building. Both front and rear exits would be blocked before he got downstairs. The roof was his only hope for escape.

Shaver grabbed up a chair and went out the door and

along the hall. He put the chair under the hatch leading to the attic. He stood on the chair and opened the hatch and drew himself up. He caught his toe in the back of the chair and pulled it up after him.

Not very good, Shaver thought, looking back at the hallway floor. A ring of dirt had fallen and marked his escape route for all to see. He shut the hatch – there was no going back now – and returned his gun to its holster. He took a penlight out of his jacket pocket and probed the inky blackness. He moved the light around the attic twice in a growing panic and then the faint beam finally fell on a ventilation opening.

If only, Shaver prayed. He picked his way across the rafters and knelt down beside it and felt himself start to breathe again. The hole was large enough for him to slip through. There was a drop of only ten feet or so to the roof of the neighboring building.

Shaver tore away the wooden slats and then turned around and squeezed through the hole feet first. He slid down face first against the rough brick wall and hung there a moment and then twisted around as he dropped to the roof. He landed in a crouch and froze that way. There was a ring of cold steel pressed against his temple. The barrel of a gun.

Twelve

'You're being just a bit overzealous, aren't you, corporal?' Petapiece asked, stepping back with his pistol. 'Your assignment was to take a chap on a short vacation. I don't recall asking that you burgle my flat.'

Shaver came slowly out of his crouch. He had been so looking forward to this meeting. But it was him, not Petapiece, who was to be pointing the gun, and a gang of killers – coming around the corner any moment now – was another script change he hadn't approved.

'Well?' Petapiece said.

'I wouldn't exactly call it a burglary.'

'More like an official police investigation, eh?' Petapiece said. 'I almost trod on your heels coming home. That was an interesting spiel you were giving my landlady ...' He motioned to the rooftops beyond. 'I had to circle around this way to avoid passing her door. She's going to scream next time she sees me.'

'I was checking on you,' Shaver admitted. It was obvious now where Petapiece had been headed. From this roof you could just grab hold of the fire-escape ladder at the rear of the tenement.

'Why?'

Shaver wondered how much time he had before another pistol was pointed at his head through the ventilator opening. That could happen any second now, and the chap with his finger on the trigger probably wouldn't stop to ask questions. He'd just pull. 'Is there someplace we can talk?'

'What's wrong with here?'

'Everything.'

'It suits me fine,' Petapiece said, smiling. He backed off a bit and sat down on the rim of a skylight. His expression indicated that he was prepared to stay all night if necessary.

'Then good-by,' Shaver told him. He stepped into the light and opened his coat and got the butt end of his Webley between thumb and forefinger. He gently pulled the gun out of its holster and lowered it to the roof and slid it across the tarred surface.

Petapiece watched this performance unsurely, his own pistol holding on Shaver's skull, his trigger finger aching with the tension. 'I could kill you . . .'

So could a number of other chaps, Shaver thought. He told himself that he was going to die for sure if he hung around much longer. So he might as well gamble on Petapiece.

'I mean it.'

'So do I,' Shaver said. He put his hands together and clasped them behind his head. He took a deep breath and started walking.

'You're out of your fucking mind,' Petapiece said harshly.

'I've always spoken highly of you,' Shaver said. He walked across the roof wondering if and when the slug would hit him. He wondered how badly it would hurt and how long it would take him to die. He wondered why he hadn't left on that trip about half an hour ago.

Goliath stood with a huge foot lifted and aimed at Petapiece's door. 'Now?' he whispered.

'No,' said the small man whose code name was Kavinsky. He pointed to the ring of dust on the hallway floor and then at the hatch in the ceiling.

Goliath studied one and then the other and finally the significance dawned on him. He put his hands together to form a step and held it in readiness.

'No,' said Kavinsky. He did not fancy being boosted up into what could well be a trap. Shaver might be sitting at the edge of the hatch with his gun at the ready. He might blow a large hole in the first head that came popping through.

'Then what?' Goliath asked.

Kavinsky was tempted to tell the giant to stick his head through the hatch. But the stupid ox might realize his motive and it wasn't wise to risk his ire. He was little better than a wild animal. He killed by instinct.

'Follow me,' Kavinsky said. He turned and ran back down the stairs.

Goliath stared after him in disbelief and then shrugged his massive shoulders and started in pursuit. If this was wrong, it wasn't his fault, he thought. It was good to have someone else making the mistakes.

Shaver went into a coffeehouse and led the way to a rear booth. He sat down and was careful to keep his hands on top of the table. Petapiece slipped in opposite him and kept one hand stuffed in his coat pocket. It still held his gun and the gun was pointed at Shaver's groin.

'What'll you have?' Shaver asked.

'Your balls, soon.'

'Relax,' Shaver told him, taking his own advice. He had made a long trip with a gun at his back and he found it much more pleasant to be facing the thing. He also felt a whole lot safer. If Petapiece wanted to kill him, he would have done it back on the roof, not followed him two blocks to a crowded coffeehouse. It also seemed apparent that the giant and his companions had been given the slip. Surely they'd have closed in by now had they spotted him?

A buxom young waitress came to their booth and Shaver ordered Irish coffee with a double shot and then looked expectantly at Petapiece.

'Just plain,' Petapiece grumbled.

'I'll buy,' Shaver said, smiling.

'Plain,' Petapiece repeated.

Shaver shrugged and enjoyed the view of the girl's departing derrière. Some farm maiden new to the city and its evil ways. Her lower forty would be planted soon enough.

'Pay attention now,' Petapiece said. 'I asked a question and I want an answer. Why?'

Shaver looked into the pale blue eyes. He thought that the wild animal might be lurking there again. But all he could detect was worry and fear.

'Answer me.'

'McDermott doesn't seem to know anything about you.'

Petapiece visibly paled. 'You discussed your assignment with him?'

'No,' Shaver said. 'How could I? He doesn't know anything about it. Yet you claimed he recommended me for the job.'

'Not personally,' Petapiece said, obviously relieved. 'When I said he spoke highly of you, I meant in written reports.'

'Oh,' Shaver said. He considered for a moment. 'There's another thing. McDermott doesn't know about my hearing going so badly for me. He thinks it's still to be held.'

'Of course,' Petapiece said. 'That's also what your commanding officer thinks. He won't learn otherwise unless you mess up – at which point he'll be advised how he can conveniently wash his hands of you.'

'Sounds plausible enough.'

'Which means . . . ?'

'It's like I said,' Shaver replied easily. 'I was checking. I wanted to find out who you are. Who you *really* are.'

Petapiece made a small snorting sound. 'You've some doubt as to my identity?'

'Yes.'

'Don't be ridiculous,' Petapiece said. 'I've recited your record front and back. I know more about you than your commanding officer. What other proof do you want of my proper connections?'

'It would be nice if you could show me an identification card. Some sort of credentials from Special Branch.'

'Wouldn't it?' Petapiece laughed. 'Jesus Christ . . .' He shook his head in disbelief. 'We spy chaps always carry proper ID. Wouldn't want to make it difficult for the enemy. How else would they know where to ship our bodies?'

'I appreciate the difficulties,' Shaver said. 'But I nevertheless want proof. Such as the name of an officer known to both of us. Someone who can personally vouch for you.'

'Like hell.'

'I insist.'

Petapiece's angry answer was cut off by the return of the waitress. He sat trying to control his temper while she served the coffee and flirted mildly with Shaver.

The colonel got out his Camel cigarettes and put one between his thick lips and lit it with his gold-filled Zippo. 'Together?' he repeated softly.

'Yes,' said Kavinsky.

'Unfortunate,' the colonel said, thinking that he could hardly be blamed. If he'd given Shaver the wrong address, the bartender might have corrected him, and any incident like that would have aroused Shaver's suspicions. So he had no choice but to give the proper address and then try to outrace him. That Shaver should be the first to arrive . . . that Petapiece should show up at this precise instant . . . that the two of them should somehow manage to slip away together . . . such were the vagaries of fate and how could he be blamed?

Samuel, sitting in the back seat of the Chrysler, stared out of the window despondently and offered no comment. He thought it strange that there was no temper tantrum now. To permit Shaver to reach Petapiece was the final, fatal error – the mistake which could scuttle the whole operation – and yet the news was accepted calmly enough. The car was not kicked to pieces. The cobblestones were not ripped up. Neighboring buildings remained intact.

'Do you think he'll confess?' the colonel asked after a while.

Samuel shrugged. Who could possibly fathom Shaver's mind? Who could predict which way a weasel might move?

The colonel thought that fate played strange tricks. This morning he had wanted nothing more in this world than for Shaver to confess. That, after all, was the whole idea, and many months of planning had led up to the moment where Shaver was supposed to confess to Petapiece and Petapiece was supposed to notify his superiors. But now, of course, Shaver knew far too much, and the added details could ruin everything, and now the worst thing that could happen was for Shaver to confess.

'If he confesses, we'll have to kill both of them, you know,' the colonel said.

Samuel said nothing. He didn't see how that would solve anything. If they were reduced to that, they might as well throw the whole thing in and start running. The operation couldn't possibly be salvaged if Petapiece died. His was one corpse too many.

'But he may not confess,' the colonel decided. He leaned back in his seat and sat smoking thoughtfully. He told himself he had never met anyone quite as unpredictable as Shaver. A truly worthy foe.

Shaver waited until the waitress had left and then challenged Petapiece. 'What's wrong?' he demanded. 'If you are what you claim to be, there's no harm proving it, is there?'

'You bloody fool,' Petapiece said, barely able to speak. 'You think there's a regular force officer within a thousand miles who knows anything about me? You think anyone I might take you to tonight could prove on demand that *he* was in Special Branch?'

Shaver sipped at his coffee. He couldn't make up his mind whether Petapiece was lying or not. 'It would be that difficult, huh?'

'With reason,' Petapiece said. 'With damn good reason.' He made an angry gesture at himself. 'Do you think I relish this role? A dirty bum ... cadging drinks ... sleeping in flophouses?'

'I had meant to ask that, too,' Shaver admitted. 'It strikes me as just a bit too much. Rather above and beyond the call.'

'Duty doesn't enter it,' Petapiece said. 'The Dirty John gimmick is my life insurance policy. It's what keeps me from harm in this filthy business – and it's what protects the men who report to me.' He pushed away his coffee and stared hatefully at Shaver. 'You've got your nerve wanting my credentials. Where are yours? – except for the most piddling of jobs?'

'Such as kidnaping CIA agents?'

'Oh,' Petapiece said, more resigned than surprised. 'So that is what's eating at your asshole. You're not so entirely stupid that you didn't finally look up your victim's background?'

Shaver didn't answer.

'Well, it's out then,' Petapiece said. 'How's that for the bitter truth? The KGB is so fucking incompetent that it puts a CIA agent on the top of its dangerous radicals list in

Canada. Ottawa is so fucking afraid of Kosygin staying home that it actually agrees to put the snatch on poor Henke. And I'm so fucking lucky that the job comes down to me for assignment.'

Shaver still didn't speak.

'I can see Ottawa's point, of course,' Petapiece said, smiling faintly. 'They couldn't very well tell the Russians that Henke is a Yankee spy. That's just not done – and besides, what if Henke's next posting is to Eastern Europe, eh? We'd have signed the bastard's death warrant.' The smile widened and he changed his mind about not wanting his coffee. 'But Ottawa was moved mainly by the idea of teaching the Yanks a badly needed lesson. They've no goddam business sending spies up here. It's time one of them got a bad scare.'

Shaver was toying with his cup. 'So it's really nothing more than a joke?'

'The bitter truth,' Petapiece said, laughing now. 'It was too much of a joke to waste one of my regular agents on. They've got more important things to do – and you were sitting on your bony arse mooning about your hearing.' The pale blue eyes twinkled over the rim of the coffee cup. 'I only did it as a favor. There's nothing boosts the spirits like a little derring-do.'

'Don't think I'm not grateful,' Shaver said, smiling in return.

'And don't think I'm not,' Petapiece said. 'You're perfect to my needs. If you come through a winner, you'll keep your job and your stripes, and you'll get a pat on the head and a transfer to Newfoundland. If you bungle it? – well, the assignment isn't really that important, and all we've sacrificed is a troublesome corporal, not a highly skilled agent worth his weight in gold.'

'Newfoundland?'

'You'd prefer the High Arctic? It doesn't really matter. Just as long as you're a few light years from my realm of operations.'

'Newfoundland sounds fine.'

'Then it's all settled?' Petapiece asked. 'Your doubts and suspicions all washed away? No need for a private audience with the Supreme High Poobah of Special Branch?' He drained his cup and returned it to the table. 'I'll tell you what. Let's you and me buy a bottle and slip over to where you're hiding Sleeping Beauty. I've no desire to go home – you've fixed me good with the landlady – and I could use a few laughs after this episode.'

'Why not?' Shaver said agreeably. He threw his coffee in the grinning face and tipped over the table.

Petapiece rolled out from under, trying to pull his gun free, but Shaver was waiting for him, his boot slamming viciously. He kicked him in the head first, and then the stomach, and finally in the shins, the last blow almost hard enough to knock the foot off.

'Sorry,' Shaver said, bending to retrieve his Webley. 'You piled it so high that my mind snapped. I think I could have managed the rest – but Newfoundland?' He was smiling agreeably once more when he turned to the stricken waitress. 'Don't worry about his bill. I'm buying for the gentleman. I always do.'

The girl screamed and Shaver pushed a couple of bills into her ample bodice and backed out through the swinging doors into the kitchen. He kept backing up, smiling at the startled help, trying to assure them that he meant no harm, and he went out the back door that way, carefully covering his retreat. He took two steps into the alley and then a giant's hands closed about his throat and he could feel himself being choked to death.

Thirteen

It was one of those rare, brilliant, incredibly beautiful moments, Colonel Vostik decided. To feel the thrill that can only come in combat. To have the desperate battle suddenly turn. To snatch victory from the jaws of seemingly certain defeat.

'How would the corporal phrase it?' Colonel Vostik asked, getting out his glass and his sour mash whiskey. 'I feel marvelous. Flipping marvelous.'

'That sounds like him, all right,' Samuel said, smiling. It was a sort of routine smile in a very ordinary kind of face. It wasn't a smile that anyone would particularly notice.

'Flipping marvelous,' Colonel Vostik repeated, enjoying himself. He tucked his glass between his stump and his stomach and poured himself about two inches of liquor. He thought that this was one occasion when it might be appropriate to offer a drink but quickly changed his mind. Drinking with the troops was unwise. It could lead to disciplinary problems.

'Just like him,' Samuel said. His looks were his fortune. It was hard to believe anyone could look quite so ordinary. You could put him in a room with half a dozen other men and later ask an agent who was present to describe the men in the room and the agent would invariably falter when trying to describe Samuel.

A door off the living room opened and a voice called softly to Colonel Vostik. 'He's ready . . .'

'Send him in then,' Vostik ordered.

'This will be interesting,' Samuel said.

'Won't it?' Vostik agreed.

Goliath finished tying the rope around the engine block and then held up the other end unsurely. 'The neck?' he asked.

'No,' said Kavinsky. 'The ankles. Both of them.'

Goliath grunted assent and tied the other end of the rope around the ankles of Detective Sergeant Hardison. 'Shall I do it now?' he asked.

'Yes,' said Kavinsky.

Goliath picked up the engine block and lifted it over his head. He walked with it to the edge of the flooded gravel pit. He flung it out into space and then stepped aside quickly to watch the swift passage of the corpse. He seemed pleased and surprised that the arrangement worked so well and that one had followed the other.

Kavinsky waited for the splash and then turned and walked down the hill to where they had parked the Chrysler. He thought that things were going rather well. Two down and one to go.

There was nothing whatsoever to fear from the woman's corpse. She was a cosmetics peddler and her route would have taken her over many blocks before she tangled with Goliath. No one had seen that encounter – if they had, the police would be at the scene, their investigation under way long ago – so there was nothing to connect her to the Polack slut's apartment building. When her body was found, miles from the scene, the police would have no idea where she had met foul play, and no way of establishing the link between her murder and that of Hardison.

Hardison, now, was a different matter, and they probably hadn't heard the last of him. Hardison may have told someone at police headquarters that he was going to the Polish slut's flat. If he had done so, that linked him not only to her, but also to Shaver, and that could raise all sorts of difficult questions. It wouldn't stop the operation. That would go ahead regardless now. But it might cast a shadow on the long-range outcome. So they could only pray that Hardison hadn't told anyone where he was going. If he hadn't told anyone, there was no harm done, and Hardison's unhappy end, if and when his body was discovered, would have a logical explanation. Some criminal had taken his revenge.

'Hurry up, dammit,' Kavinsky said. He slipped behind the wheel of the Chrysler and started the motor and sat waiting impatiently. He told himself that it wasn't fair that he should always be the one to correct the giant's mistakes.

Goliath came striding down the hill. He liked it best when there was someone to give orders. If there had been someone to give orders, he might not have killed the police sergeant, he thought. But it really wasn't his fault. What else could he have done? Hardison had surprised him in the flat and there had been no time to think. Shaver was already coming up the front steps of the building. It was too much to think of all at once. No wonder he had panicked. No wonder he killed and ran.

It was the same with the cosmetics woman, Goliath thought. She also had taken him by surprise. It was too much to think of all at once. Far, far too much.

Goliath got into the car and closed the door behind him. 'What next?' he asked.

'We go back for the Polack slut,' Kavinsky said.

Goliath nodded happily. He liked it best when there was someone to give orders.

Shaver found himself standing in the living room of a strange house. He was still groggy from the aftereffects of a drug. His mind worked very slowly and his vision was blurred and it was difficult for him to walk properly.

'Good evening,' Colonel Vostik said. 'I trust you'll remember me. The gentleman who was so helpful?'

Shaver stared at him through a shimmering red mist. He could remember kicking Petapiece. He could remember stuffing the money into the girl's dress and backing out through the swinging doors. He could remember thinking that he'd had it now and that the grubby mooch probably was in Special Branch. That he'd taken his revenge and that he had no choice now but to run to the nearest telephone and confess all to McDermott . . .

'We met at The Stump Club.'

Shaver wished the red mist would go away. The figure looming through it seemed familiar. The shiny, shaved skull. The hand cut off halfway up the forearm. 'The dart player . . .'

'That's correct,' Vostik said. 'You were asking for the

address of Commander Petapiece and I was kind enough to supply it. I wanted to help you then, and I still do, of course. That's why I've had you brought here. My only interest is to help.'

Shaver rubbed at his throat. He could remember the giant's hands squeezing the life out of him. The giant had almost killed him. Now the dart player wanted to help him. It didn't make sense.

'My apologies,' Vostik said sympathetically. 'Goliath doesn't realize his own strength. He's also apt to get excited at times. He just gets so eager – to help.'

Shaver tried very hard to concentrate. There was some connection between the giant and the dart player. One worked for the other and they were both his enemies and they didn't want to help at all. The dart player was lying. He was making a joke about helping. He was the leader of these men . . . the fanatics who were plotting . . .

Vostik finished his drink and set the glass aside. 'Permit me to introduce myself. My name is Colonel Muno Vostik – and I'm a member of the KGB.'

Shaver stared at him dully. That really didn't make any sense. The KGB?

Vostik snapped his fingers and pointed at the tape recorder on the coffee table. 'Play it again, Sam.'

Samuel got up and turned on the tape. Shaver recognized the two tinny voices. One of them belonged to Petapiece. The other was his own – and that was his laughter now.

'This dear little flower? A threat to Kosygin?'

'Seriously. Henke's the top man on the KGB surveillance list drawn up for Kosygin's visit. They want Henke out of circulation the whole time Kosygin is in Canada.'

'The whole time?'

'That's right. The full eight days . . .'

The plain-looking man punched the tape and let it advance at high speed to a pre-selected spot. Shaver heard himself asking the fateful question.

'What did you have in mind?'

'Well. I'd hoped that would be apparent by now. Your job is to see that this Henke is indeed taken out of circulation.'

'Plain enough. But that wasn't the question. I meant to ask how?'

'Your problem . . .'

Samuel stopped the tape and returned to his chair.

'Your problem,' Vostik mimicked. 'Your problem, no problem.' He eased up onto a bar stool and lit another cigarette. 'You said so yourself, didn't you, corporal? "This little flower?" – "You've got a deal. Consider it done." '

Shaver didn't answer.

'How would you phrase it, corporal?' Vostik asked. 'A lead-pipe cinch? A little flower free for the plucking . . . ?' He let the smoke drift lazily from his wide, flattened nostrils. 'I assume you were successful in your mission?'

Shaver still didn't reply.

'Play it again, Sam,' Vostik ordered, leaning against the bar. He couldn't remember when he had enjoyed himself so much. This was marvelous. Flipping marvelous.

Samuel got up and advanced the tape to another pre-selected place.

'Resourceful, you are,' Petapiece was saying. 'You know your business and you'll be doing it right. Henke's fast asleep in some basement room. You're keeping him that way with an injection every few hours . . . Tell me. Where have you got him stashed?'

Shaver could vaguely recall the scene. This was where he was pulling his hand free from Petapiece.

'You're right,' Petapiece was saying. 'It's your dark secret, isn't it? There's no one you dare tell,' and then Shaver could hear himself answering, 'My sentiments exactly.'

Vostik sat smoking and watching Shaver. He thought again that this was one of those incredibly beautiful moments. Something to hold and to cherish. 'I don't share Commander Petapiece's blind confidence,' he said softly. 'Dark secrets aren't my cup of tea. I want proof that a job is done.'

Shaver was still looking at the tape recorder. 'Proof?'

'That's right,' Vostik said. 'I want you to take me to Henke. I want to see him with my own eyes.'

'Well,' Shaver said, his glib tongue gone. 'I'm sure that can be arranged. But there's proper channels . . .'

'You lying bastard,' Vostik screamed, pounding the bar. 'You sniveling, pitiful coward.' The blood rushed to his heavy, blunt face and his thick lips lifted like a vicious, snarling dog's. 'Admit it. You bungled the job.'

Shaver pulled back involuntarily. Vostik's sudden wild screams had hit like a physical blow.

'Admit it, damn you,' Vostik shouted. He pushed down off his stool and slapped Shaver across the face. 'Admit it. You bungled the job.'

Shaver could only twist away awkwardly. His reflexes were still too numb to attempt any defense. He went reeling backward across the room under the onslaught of Vostik's whiplike blows. Finally he fell to his hands and knees and resigned himself to the beating.

Vostik grabbed him by the back of the neck and pulled him to his feet. He twisted his arm behind his back and marched him downstairs. He pushed through a door into a small bedroom.

Shaver stared in disbelief. Henke was laid out carefully on the bed.

Vostik's voice was soft and caressing. 'Resourceful, you are, corporal. Henke's fast asleep in some basement room. You're keeping him that way with an injection every few hours ...'

Shaver thought that this was all far beyond his understanding.

'I told you I wanted to help,' Vostik said.

Bogna paid off the taxi driver and buttoned her coat against the chill night wind. She thought again that she didn't have the nerve to go up to her flat. Discovering the same corpse twice in one evening was a bit much.

Nor did it help, she told herself, staring after the departing cab, to have blundered into a sordid murder movie as her excuse for arriving home late. She'd have walked out on the damn thing if it hadn't been for the fear of the police asking her to recount the film's plot.

A man came by, out for a casual stroll, it seemed, but Bogna had the feeling that he was looking at her strangely. It was all that she could do not to break and run.

'Good evening,' the man said, smiling and touching his hat. He walked on past and didn't look back.

Bogna thought that her nerves couldn't stand it if she went up to her flat and that it really wasn't necessary to torture herself. Why go through the motions of 'discovering' Hardison's body when all she had to do was start screaming in the hall?

That would seem logical enough. The police wouldn't expect a woman to remain in her flat and calmly telephone them the news of a body in her bathroom. They'd expect her to run out and slam the door behind her and go screaming to a neighbor or the building superintendent. So why bother to go upstairs at all? Why not just start screaming?

Bogna wondered why she hadn't thought of this solution earlier. It would have saved her a lot of needless worry all through the movie. She started toward the front door of her apartment building and then stopped abruptly. What if someone had removed Hardison's body in her absence? What if the murderer had returned to the scene of the crime?

Oh, God, Bogna thought. She *had* to make sure Hardison was still in her flat. If she called the police and they came and found him gone . . . ?

But if that was possible, then she also risked running into the killer, didn't she? What if he was waiting for her to come home? What if . . . ?

Bogna saw that the man who had passed her on the sidewalk had now turned around and was looking at her strangely. He was very definitely looking at her strangely.

Oh, God, Bogna thought.

Shaver sat at a card table with a pen in his hand and a blank sheet of paper before him.

'How would you begin, Corporal?' Vostik asked, pacing the living room. 'Sir? Dear Sir? Dear Commander?' He stopped and considered carefully. 'You wouldn't use his alias in the salutation?'

'Sir, I think, would be most appropriate,' Shaver said.

Samuel nodded approvingly.

'Sir, then,' Vostik said, resuming his pacing. 'That part is settled on. What next?'

'I regret to inform you,' Shaver suggested.

Vostik glanced at Samuel and he again nodded his approval. Samuel had a great number of specialties. He was especially proficient in English.

Sir, Shaver wrote, anxious to get it over with. *I regret to inform you that I failed in my assignment. Henke was already gone when I broke into his flat. It seems apparent that he faked his own kidnaping and that he remains free and poses a threat to Kosygin. I misled you and pretended to have him in custody in the hope I might be able to locate him before Kosygin's arrival. I realize now that this is futile and I am advising you of the true facts of the situation so that you will have ample time to provide additional protection for the Russian premier.*

> *Respectfully,*
> *Cpl. Timothy Shaver*

Vostik stood silently watching until Shaver had completed the letter. He picked it up and read it with the sort of apprehensive expression one might expect to see on a sapper picking his way through a mine field. He frowned and passed it to Samuel.

'I think you'll find it suitable,' Shaver said.

'Perfect,' Samuel agreed. He passed it back to Vostik.

'You're being strangely co-operative,' Vostik said.

'I told you I wanted to help,' Shaver said.

Vostik smiled and folded the letter and put it in the envelope which had already been addressed by Shaver. He decided that he had been wrong in his initial assessment. Shaver demonstrated cunning only when he was scrambling to save his own hide. He was truly a fool under any other circumstances.

Shaver put the top back on the pen and positioned it in the middle of the card table. He decided that he had fallen into the hands of the Russian version of the Keystone Cops. They were the damndest bunch of idiots he had ever run across. Nothing they did or said made any sense whatsoever.

Vostik sealed the envelope and put it in his pocket. He crossed to the bar and eased up onto a stool. He clutched his glass with his stump and poured the usual two inches of whiskey and then lit a Camel with his gold-filled Zippo. None of this was natural to him – neither the mannerisms nor the trappings – but he had practiced them so often that it would seem strange to act himself.

'Let me tell you a story,' Vostik said. 'Remember the German generals who plotted against Hitler? They wanted him dead – so they could negotiate a peace with the Allies.'

Shaver suddenly had a strange feeling in his stomach. He wondered if he had been wrong about the letter. He had thought it so stupid and harmless to anyone but himself.

'We've got much the same situation now,' Vostik said, sipping at his whiskey. 'The same but different. It's backward. Reversed ...' He paused to savor Shaver's shattered look. 'Some Russian generals want Kosygin dead – so that he can't establish a détente with the West.'

Shaver turned away and silently cursed himself. He was such a bloody fool, he thought. Such a poor dumb bugger.

'It's very difficult to kill Kosygin in Russia,' Vostik said. 'His security is fantastic there and the chances of failure are very high. So are the chances of being caught. But here?' He smiled and sipped happily at his drink. 'This is an ideal place to have it done. Your security is lax and the chances of being caught are remote. But the most appealing aspect, of course, is the opportunity not only to escape, but also to escape blame.'

Shaver tried to close his mind to what was coming. He didn't want to hear any more. He wanted to die in peace and ignorance.

'The blame will fall on Henke,' Vostik said. 'There'll be ample proof of his guilt – and there also will be evidence that the KGB repeatedly warned the RCMP that Henke posed a threat to our exalted Premier. Can the KGB be faulted if the Canadian police failed to take proper precautions? This, after all, is Canadian, not Russian, soil. The KGB can do just so much. It argued against the visit. It even tried its best to block the trip. But when the know-it-all politicians override the police ... ?'

Samuel coughed discreetly. He didn't think it wise to go into quite so much detail.

'We visualize something parallel to the Warren Commission investigation of the Kennedy assassination,' Vostik continued, ignoring the interruption. 'It will bring out Henke's minor association with the CIA and the obvious fact that many other persons had to be involved in such a large and expensively mounted undertaking. There will be the implicit suggestion that the operation was planned, organized, and financed by some fanatical right-wing element in the United States, which knew and took advantage of Henke's hatred of Russia. There will be the lingering suspicion that if one could only follow the twisted trail back far enough it would lead to the doorstep of the CIA.'

Samuel coughed again and was again ignored.

'It's a brilliant plan,' Vostik said. 'Complex, daring, subtle. A masterpiece of intrigue that would shame the gods . . .' He put his glass aside and slipped down off his stool. 'Have you any conception of the worries and troubles you've brought me? Have you any idea of how close you came to creating a shambles?'

Shaver stared back at him miserably. It looked as if the colonel was becoming angry again.

'I was completely baffled at first,' Vostik said. 'You made your report to Petapiece and he just sat there laughing. Quoting from the newspaper and laughing . . .' He hit his forehead with the heel of his hand. 'I thought we had done something wrong. I thought it was *our* fault.'

'That's all resolved now,' Samuel said.

'Yes,' Vostik admitted, finally acknowledging the warnings. He thought that perhaps the precise details of the plan should remain unspoken. It was enough that Shaver realized beyond any doubt that the plan would succeed. Despite Shaver's impossible behavior – the plan would succeed.

'Your duty was so clear and simple,' Vostik complained, turning back to Shaver. 'It required only that you tell the truth. All you had to do was report back to Petapiece and admit that you bungled.' He shook his head and sighed. 'You can see that your admission is a small but important part of the plot, can't you, Corporal? We require a small security flap just prior to Kosygin's arrival. Nothing so serious as to stop the visit or alter the schedule. The kind of thing that will appear very minor now – but loom large as death when it's time to collect the evidence and assess the blame.'

Vostik took Shaver's letter from his pocket and held it up tauntingly. 'Here's the pebble that will spread the small ripples of concern,' he said, smiling. 'Special Branch will be more embarrassed than anything else. It knows Henke is with the CIA and can't possibly pose a threat to Kosygin, but the KGB, however mistakenly, did request specific action – and so there'll be some red faces at having fumbled such a simple request. Special Branch will apologize to the KGB, minimizing the thing as much as possible, and the KGB, making its first "mistake," will decide that the RCMP knows what it is doing. Kosygin's visit will proceed as planned.'

Shaver braced himself for the rest of it. He knew there was one final flourish. Vostik's wolfish grin guaranteed that.

'Can anyone fault the KGB?' Vostik asked. 'Not really. Not under the circumstances. Not when we can turn your cowardice to our advantage . . .' He put the letter back in his pocket. 'The KGB officer who makes this fateful error will testify at the subsequent hearing that he was misled by the RCMP. He'll swear that a high-ranking officer told him confidentially that Henke obviously had been killed by Corporal Shaver. The KGB official will confess that he was sadly taken in by this story which later proved – with such tragic consequences – to be utterly false.'

Vostik's blunt face was shining with anticipation. 'Now. Shall we review the three final phases in the life and times of Corporal Timothy Shaver? Phase One: In a desperate attempt to save himself, the corporal at first pretends that he has been successful in his assignment, deliberately misleading his superior. Phase Two: Unable to locate Henke, concerned about Kosygin's safety, and realizing that he will be called upon to produce Henke once Kosygin leaves Canada, the corporal sends a letter to his superior confessing that he has bungled and suggesting that Henke has faked his own disappearance. Phase Three: Overcome by guilt and remorse, the poor corporal, knowing his career has been ruined, commits suicide.'

Shaver managed to accept the news without flinching. He had the advantage of knowing well in advance. He had been plainly marked for death the moment Vostik began his story.

Nor was there any use praying for miracles, Shaver thought bitterly. Petapiece and Special Branch would view his letter exactly as predicted. There'd be no brilliant deductions as to the truth of the matter. No last-minute cavalry charge to save the day.

Shaver thought that the only hope at all lay with Bogna. If she survived the night; if the police took her into custody when she called them; if at noon tomorrow she told them everything she knew – and especially about how much they could learn in the Books of Knowledge.

Shaver had no sooner fashioned these thoughts when there was the sound of an auto driving into the carport. A few moments later Kavinsky entered the house with Bogna. He pushed her into the middle of the living room and gave Vostik the message Shaver had left hidden under F for Fables.

Vostik glanced at it and smiled. 'It seems I was mistaken. We'll have to make that a double suicide.'

Bogna stared at Shaver with tear-bruised eyes. 'I'm sorry ...'

Shaver had no answer for her. He had no answer for anything now. No answers at all.

Fourteen

Colonel Vostik began his final inspection tour the next morning by driving upcoast to a small private airfield on a ranch a short distance north of Squamish at the head of Howe Sound. In a tightly guarded hangar there he examined a helicopter which had been repainted to resemble the helicopter operated by the Vancouver Police Department. He compared the fake machine with photographs of the real one and pronounced himself completely satisfied.

It was a shame that the American killer, who had been imported specifically to become a corpse, would not be a passenger, serving as one more piece of 'evidence' pointing to the United States when the helicopter's wreckage was found. But what was done was done – that was the price of risking the dandy against Shaver – and they could manage without him. It might even be better this way. More subtle.

Vostik put the loss from his mind and spoke at length with the pilot of the helicopter about radio communications, the scheduled takeoff time, the route to be flown, the pickup arrangements, the holding position, the approach to the city, and the exact altitude of the final run. He questioned the KGB veteran very closely on all aspects of his mission – placing special emphasis on the crucial final moments – and then shook hands with him and wished him well. During this meeting he referred to the helicopter pilot as Fat Boy.

Driving back to Vancouver, the colonel remarked that the chances for the operation's success appeared excellent, and Samuel, sitting beside him in the back seat of the Chrysler, gravely agreed that this was so. He didn't believe this but saw no reason to tinker with the colonel's ebullient mood.

Samuel knew from experience – as Vostik also knew, if he

cared to admit it – that any number of things could go wrong before the day was through. Even now, he thought, certain men would be meeting and talking, and they would be putting their minds to certain questions. If they had pedestrian minds, all was well. But if they had leaping, soaring, convoluted minds, the shit might very well hit the fan.

One of the principals at one of these meetings was a fat, balding, untidy man named Ferguson who supposedly was the manager of Ace Novelty Imports, but who actually functioned as British Columbia liaison for Special Branch. As the Chrysler sped back to the city, Ferguson was reading the letter signed by Shaver, which had been delivered about a half hour earlier to Petapiece. After he had read it for the third time, Ferguson flattened the letter out on his desk, carefully pressing out all the creases, and his face was a study in mixed emotions when he finally looked up at his unexpected visitor.

This, Ferguson thought, was an awfully bad show, but at the same time it couldn't happen to a better bastard. 'You've been properly diddled, haven't you, Commander?' Ferguson said.

Petapiece nodded unhappily. He was being careful not to speak unless it was absolutely necessary. The simple act of breathing was torture enough.

'It's not something I can sit on,' Ferguson said, as if to suggest the thought had crossed his mind. 'I'll have to get on the blower to Ottawa right away.' He looked at his watch and noted that the recipient of his call would be back from lunch in precisely eight minutes. 'Taggart will be displeased.'

How like Ferguson to rub it in, Petapiece thought, grimacing. He had the world's worst headache, four cracked ribs, and a broken ankle – and still the bugger wasn't satisfied.

'It's all most unusual,' Ferguson said, pushing up from his desk. 'Most unusual indeed.' He crossed to his office door and checked to make sure that it was locked. 'Whatever possessed you to assign this corporal in the first place?'

'I've explained that,' Petapiece said.

'Oh yes,' Ferguson sighed. 'I forgot. You're short of agents, as always, and the job *wasn't important*, quote unquote, and you enjoy a lark once in a while.'

'I never called it a lark,' Petapiece protested.

'No,' Ferguson admitted, returning to his desk. 'But Taggart will think that. You know Taggart will think that ...' He almost permitted himself a small smile of pleasure. 'I'm sorry, old chap. I shouldn't be questioning your judgment, should I? You're the field commander, after all, and who am I, really? Just one of the bum boys at divisional level. I don't give the orders. I only take them and pass them along.'

Petapiece made no comment.

'That is the proper term, isn't it?' Ferguson inquired. 'I'm sure I recall you using it the last time you went over my head. Bum boy.'

Petapiece still said nothing.

'Taggart will have to tell the KGB,' Ferguson said, looking at his watch again. 'It will be most embarrassing for him. Most embarrassing indeed.' He pushed back his chair and put his feet up on his desk. He had five more minutes before he placed the call and he might as well relax, he decided. Relax and enjoy himself. 'That's one conversation I'd like to have a tap on.'

Petapiece clenched his teeth against the searing pain in his chest. This was so like Ferguson. So goddam typical.

'There's no calling off the visit, of course,' Ferguson said, examining the ceiling. 'It's too late for that. Kosygin's plane left Moscow long ago ...' He sighed contentedly. 'But you can damn well bet that the KGB will have the final say in security from this moment on. It'll be their show now – not Taggart's.'

Petapiece thought that he didn't have to take this crap. He didn't have to take it for one more lousy minute.

'Can you imagine the bill they'll run up?' Ferguson mused. 'Double the guards at every stop. Building checks. Rooftop patrols ...' His face glowed with pleasure. 'And for what? To stave off a fat little sex pervert in the employ of our good neighbor to the south.'

Petapiece made up his mind to leave. He had dragged himself in, half dead with the pain, and he'd done his duty, distasteful as it was, and he didn't have to take crap.

'You better stick around,' Ferguson said. 'There's the off-chance Taggart will want to talk to you. He may have some questions. Or instructions.' He glanced at his watch and saw that he had only two minutes to go. 'As a matter of fact, I've got a question myself, old chap. Where's Henke?'

Petapiece dropped back into his chair.

'You know what I think?' Ferguson said. 'I think Henke spotted Shaver following him. I think Henke realized we had him under some sort of investigation and decided that he'd have a bit of fun with us. The puddle of blood . . . the broken window . . . the footsteps out back – I'll bet it was Henke, not Shaver, who contrived that evidence of foul play, and can you imagine Shaver's face when he broke into the flat and found it?'

Petapiece's mind was finally functioning. For some reason – because of the pain, or, perhaps, because he had been trying to blot out the entire disaster – that fateful question simply hadn't occurred to him. *Where is Henke?*

'I think I'd better talk to Taggart,' Petapiece said.

'Sure,' Ferguson said, picking up the phone. 'That's fine by me, but I wouldn't want to bet on Taggart.' He was smiling as he dialed into the direct long-distance trunk. 'What makes you think you'll be on speaking terms after he hears Shaver's letter?'

Petapiece hoped Taggart wouldn't react so stupidly. But he had to admit it might happen.

Vostik's next stop was at the Hotel Vancouver where, several weeks before, the resident manager, upon receiving a telephone call from External Affairs in Ottawa, had reserved an entire wing of the tenth floor for 'A. Kosygin & Party.'

Vostik met with two more KGB agents, one of them an electronics expert renowned for his calm, cool manner under pressure, the other a particularly adept car driver. In their talk, which dealt mainly with radio communications and the Datsun 240Z which had replaced the Rover, Vostik referred to the first man as Eagle Eye and to the other as Snooper.

Eagle Eye reported that his compact but high-powered

radio equipment had come through admirably. He had made satisfactory contact with Fat Boy at Squamish and contact would improve when the chopper was in flight and closer to Vancouver. Snooper's test transmissions from the 240Z at the airport had been loud and clear in the middle of the day. In the evening they would be that much better.

Vostik said he wished the transmitter in his Chrysler had half that range and Eagle Eye remarked that it was just as well that it didn't. He wanted no one but himself giving instructions once the operation got under way. Otherwise a crucial order might be blocked out and go unheard. The colonel was angered by the remark – he didn't feel such a reminder was necessary – but managed to control his temper. While the agent's manner provoked, it was a small price to pay for someone so very, very dependable under pressure.

Vostik then returned to the lobby and had a leisurely lunch in the Timber Club. He ordered the Oysters Florentine and suggested the same dish to Samuel, who had been a silent witness at the meeting upstairs. Samuel agreed, and he even ate all his spinach, despite the fact that he had hated the stuff since childhood.

Vostik remarked after lunch that only a miracle could stop them now, and Samuel accepted this proposition with the same stoic deference that he had managed with the Oysters Florentine. He gave no outward sign – but he found it hard to swallow.

Meetings were taking place. Men were talking to other men. Minds were at work . . .

Inspector McDermott hung up the telephone and opened the bottom drawer in his desk. He took out a roll of teletype paper and tucked it under his arm. He got up and went out his door and down the hall a few paces and in another door. 'Have you got a moment?' he asked pleasantly.

'Sure,' Sub-Inspector Benson said.

'I just got a call from Ottawa,' McDermott said, sitting down. 'Taggart at Special Branch. It seems he's had one of our chaps in his employ.'

'Oh?' Benson said, eyeing the teletype roll. 'Who might that be?'

'Corporal Shaver.'

'*Shaver?*'

'My reaction,' McDermott said, smiling. 'My reaction exactly.' He put the teletype roll on Benson's desk. 'You remember Henke? The one mentioned in dispatches? The CIA's resident sex fiend? It's a long, long story, but Shaver was assigned to sit on him for a while.'

'Whatever for?'

'For no good reason,' McDermott said. 'Of that you can be assured. But then you know Special Branch.'

Benson reached for the teletype roll. 'I take it our security leak is solved?'

'Yes,' McDermott said. 'It's obvious now what happened. Shaver wanted some background info on Henke. He was persona non grata around here, so he asked Kirchoff to pull the file. She did so – and made the mistake of using my name on a day I wasn't here.'

Benson noted that his own role in the drama had somehow been forgotten.

'As might be expected, Shaver fouled up the assignment,' McDermott said. 'Henke got away on him and then he had a terrible brawl with his Special Branch control. Knocked the chap down and literally kicked the stuffing out of him.'

'No . . .'

'Yes,' McDermott said. 'So now we know what happened to Kirchoff. That's also obvious now. She's gone and run off with Shaver.' He stood up smiling radiantly. 'I venture we've seen the last of that pair.'

Benson sighed. A sad ending to a sad story. There weren't that many D cups in the world.

It wasn't until later that Benson realized he had misunderstood the inspector's last remark. The inspector had been talking about the two of them, Shaver and Kirchoff, not those huge boobs, which meant the inspector thought he had seen the last of Shaver.

Benson wondered if this was perhaps wishful thinking. He didn't like tidy packages. They made him suspicious. He thought that the matter required further investigation and that he just might take it on himself. On the other hand, though, that was going against all his natural instincts, which dictated that he strenuously avoid as much work as possible.

Benson sat thinking. This needed due consideration. One should never act rashly.

The last stop on Vostik's inspection tour was at a pleasant bungalow on Sentinel Hill, only a few miles from his own base of operations, which was in a rented house on the West Vancouver waterfront approximately halfway between Lions Gate Bridge and Fisherman's Cove. The owner of the bungalow was a comfortably retired widower who had made a small fortune upon the sale of several retail stores specializing in electronic equipment. His hobby – his passion – was photography.

This man, whose name was Mueller, was a post-war immigrant to Canada from West Germany, where he had served briefly as an *agent-provocateur* for the U.S.S.R. But that had been a quarter of a century ago and now no one would ever think to question Mueller's commitment to his adopted country. He was a model citizen in every regard, was deeply involved in several important community projects, and was under consideration as the Progressive Conservative candidate for Coast-Capilano in the next federal election.

Vostik spent almost an hour talking to Mueller. The topic was photography.

As the Chrysler drove down from Sentinel Hill, the colonel remarked that not even a miracle could stop them now, and Samuel, for the first time that day, spoke what he truly felt in his heart. He said he thought the chances for the operation's success appeared excellent.

This late in the game, if there were other minds at work, they'd better be especially brilliant. It really would take a leaping, soaring mind to stop them now.

'Damn,' said Inspector O'Brien, who was head of the Homicide Squad, Vancouver City Police Department. 'Damn and double damn.' He pushed a button on his intercom. 'I need five minutes to think, Mary.'

'Yessir,' said his secretary, who was of the persuasion that he needed a lot more than that.

O'Brien got out his pad of legal paper and made a list of

all the cases that were currently under investigation by Detective Sergeant Hardison. They came to eight in all, of which six were actually murder cases, the other two involving persons who had gone missing under suspicious circumstances.

Once this was done, O'Brien crossed out those cases that, on the basis of the facts as he knew them, could not reasonably have a bearing on the strange disappearance of the officer laughingly referred to as his ace investigator. That left him with two murder cases and one missing-persons case. The names of the two murder victims were Mounce and Wimsey. The name of the missing person was Henke.

O'Brien thumbed through the file folders piled on his desk and removed the three he had settled upon. He read the Mounce file first and then the Wimsey. Neither contained the elements he considered essential. He crossed them off his list and opened the file on Henke.

This, O'Brien decided, slowing down his reading pace, was a bit more like it. Suspected pervert. No visible means of support. Killed in his flat, or so the amount of spilled blood indicated, and then, for some strange reason, the killers removed his corpse. A tricky maneuver down a vertical fire-escape ladder. Nobody would do that unless they wanted the body awfully bad. And what good was a dead body?

Well, O'Brien thought. Perverts attract perverts, and some perverts hanker for the cold ones, don't they? The moldier the better for the furry fungus fuckers. A bad lot indeed for an innocent police sergeant to go provoking.

O'Brien closed the file and got out his pipe and spent a long time filling it to the proper specifications. He had it down to a science and served as a model for many of his men. You could always spot an O'Brien fan. They spent forever filling their pipes.

'Hmmm,' O'Brien said, examining his handiwork. He wondered if he should pull out all the stops on Hardison. Put him on the official missing-persons list. Notify all other police agencies. Mention the link to Henke. Or should he let it simmer on the back burner a while longer?

O'Brien thought that this was a difficult decision to make. Hardison could very well be off somewhere on a royal drunk, and pushing the panic button could be embarrassing to everyone, Hardison included. Besides, even if Hardison had met foul play, all the rushing in the world wouldn't help him at this stage. That meant there could be only one reason for hurrying. To nail those responsible – *if* a crime had been committed.

Decisions, decisions, O'Brien thought. He had to weigh the possible embarrassment against the time lost. *If* it was being lost.

He sighed and pushed the button on his intercom. 'Give me a bit longer, Mary.'

'Yessir,' said his secretary, who had reached that decision long ago.

Colonel Vostik returned to base extremely pleased and happy with his inspection tour. Samuel had ample proof of his high spirits. It was always a sure sign when the colonel whistled 'The Glow-Worm.'

Vostik carried in the liquor himself and unwrapped the bottles and set them on the bar. A bottle of vodka for the troops (an exception to mark this day of all days). Dickel's Sour Mash bourbon for himself. Something Special for the cowardly corporal and his Polack slut.

'We're ready,' Vostik said. Kavinsky nodded and motioned to Goliath and the two of them went downstairs.

'Three more hours,' Vostik said.

Samuel nodded and sat down.

'Three more hours,' Vostik repeated. He held his arms outstretched, pretending he was an airplane, and he started running around the living room that way, making the sounds of the engine.

Samuel sat watching and smiling.

'Rrrr,' Vostik cried, circling the room. 'Rrrrrr. Rrrrrr . . .' Suddenly he veered and dived headlong into the sofa. 'Kaboom!'

Samuel laughed and applauded.

'Marvelous,' Vostik said, pushing to his feet. 'Flipping marvelous . . .' He became aware of the presence of Shaver and Bogna. He grinned and motioned eagerly with his stump. 'Come in, come in. We're having a party.'

Fifteen

'If you insist,' Shaver said, rubbing at his bony wrists. He had awakened from a drugged sleep a half hour before to find himself spread-eagled in bed, wrists and ankles bound to the four posts, and his desperate struggles to free himself had only served to tighten his bonds, cutting off circulation to his hands and feet.

'Oh, but I don't insist,' Vostik said, crossing to the bar. 'No one is forcing a party on you. Least of all us . . .' He started opening the bottles of liquor. 'The choice is entirely up to you.'

'What choice?' Shaver asked warily. He took Bogna by the arm and led her to a sofa. She was still half sedated by the drug and moved like a zombie. She was only vaguely aware of her surroundings and of what was happening.

'Between methods of suicide,' Vostik explained, still the beaming host. 'Do you prefer to stick your service revolver in your mouth and blow the top of your head off? Or would you rather get stinking drunk and drive a car over a cliff?'

'There's no sense being an old party poop,' Shaver decided. He got Bogna seated and was going to join her on the sofa when he saw that he was being motioned away to another chair. He nodded and did as indicated.

'A happy decision,' Vostik said. 'I had hoped to have your company for a convivial hour or so.' He put a glass between his stump and stomach and filled it with Something Special. 'Why part on bad terms?'

Why indeed? Shaver thought. He noted that the seating arrangement had him effectively surrounded. Vostik was to his right, Samuel to the left, Kavinsky directly across from him, and Goliath was hovering – ready to pounce, probably – somewhere behind.

'It's been a most productive day,' Vostik went on, filling a second glass with the scotch. 'I inspected the troops and found them fit and eager for battle. Even the prophets of doom among us are sensing victory.' He delivered one of the drinks to Shaver and put the other on the coffee table in front of Bogna. 'Isn't that right, Sam?'

'Yes,' Samuel admitted.

Vostik went back to the bar and poured three two-inch shots of vodka which he ceremoniously passed around to his subordinates. Then he poured the same amount of bourbon whiskey for himself and raised his glass in a toast. 'To victory,' he said, tossing it back.

'To victory,' the others echoed, their vodka also disappearing in one long draught.

Vostik took the vodka bottle and walked around the room, pouring each man a second drink, and then returned to the bar and spilled the rest down the sink. He served himself again and emptied the bourbon bottle down the drain. The only liquor remaining was Something Special.

Samuel felt himself relax. The chances for a successful operation remained excellent.

'Drink up, Corporal,' Vostik told Shaver.

Shaver picked up his glass. There was one thing to be thankful for, he thought. He wouldn't be going out with cheap booze on his breath.

Commander Petapiece was already drunk. He had been drinking all day and he planned to go on drinking until they closed The Stump Club. He planned to get so impossibly stinking drunk that it wouldn't do just to call a taxi for him. They were going to have to call an ambulance.

For at least the hundredth time, Petapiece told himself that it was impossible, absolutely and completely impossible, for Taggart to have treated him in such a cavalier manner. Taggart's final comment in their brief telephone conversation that morning wouldn't leave his mind. It was stained on his memory. Luminous, pulsating, indelible.

If you want the pervert that badly, find him yourself, Pet.

The nerve of the son of a bitch, Petapiece thought. The colossal, mind-bending, turd-wrenching nerve. Pet, was it? Pet?

Petapiece drained his glass and slammed it on the table. The son of a bitch would live to rue his impudence, and the reckoning could come tonight. It was all very well to laugh and ridicule and make smart-ass remarks but that didn't answer the question. Where was Henke?

Until he had the answer, Taggart walked a tightrope, Petapiece thought, returning to another familiar theme. He walked a tightrope and there wasn't any net and no one to break his fall. One slip and he perished.

Petapiece couldn't articulate his fears – he had passed that several hours ago – but he knew that it was stupid and dangerous to brush over the inexplicable. In the beginning, of course, Henke had been a joke, and no one could be faulted for not taking him seriously. But Henke stopped being a joke the moment he disappeared. He became a question mark then. He became a puzzle and a mystery and a nagging doubt. He became a threat.

Yes, Petapiece decided. That wasn't putting it too strongly. A threat did loom and it could portend the worst kind of bloody disaster, and there was no way he could help avert it. The thing was out of his hands and rested with Taggart and the army of bum boys who ran Special Branch. Petapiece smiled and shook his head and thought it strange that perhaps the only man even vaguely aware of the danger was a virtual cripple getting helplessly drunk so that he could be taken home in an ambulance.

Colonel Vostik had been keeping a careful eye on his watch and now at last it was seven o'clock. The party was over, and it was time to say good-by. Farewell forever to the cowardly corporal.

'I'm afraid this is where we part,' he said, checking the amount of liquor left in the bottle of Something Special. 'There's work to be done . . .' He smiled as his eyes moved from the bottle to Shaver. 'Appointments to keep.'

'Don't hurry on my account,' Shaver said thickly.

Vostik's smile faded. It would have been better if his victim wasn't drunk, he thought. When you dulled his senses, you dulled his fear, and you also subtracted from your own pleasure.

'Isn't there something you'd like to tell me?' Shaver said, repeating a question he'd asked several times already. 'Wouldn't you like to divulge the details of your plot? Brag about how clever you are?'

Samuel didn't like the expression on the colonel's face. 'It's getting late . . .'

'You could at least explain your airplane act,' Shaver complained. 'Why the crash? You got a kamikaze pilot?'

Vostik was tempted to detail the plot – if only to spite Samuel – but decided there would be no pleasure in that either. Shaver was too far gone to appreciate the plan. He was a drunk babbling the same questions over and over.

'Come on,' Shaver said. 'How about it? You got a kamikaze?'

'Do it now,' Vostik ordered brusquely, turning away.

Kavinsky nodded and motioned to Goliath. The giant took hold of Shaver and pulled him to his feet and marched him to the door. Kavinsky followed with Bogna. Shaver tried to pull free, but his coordination was a shambles and he was helpless in the giant's viselike grip. He had consumed almost half a bottle of uncut liquor over a one-hour period and that made him drunk by anyone's reckoning. He slurred his words, he staggered when he walked, he had the feeling that he was going to throw up or pass out at any moment, but he nonetheless was very much aware of what was happening. He had determined from the start that some small part of his mind would remain clear and he had achieved this by sheer force of will and now he saw himself and his situation with a terrible mirror-image clarity.

The door opened onto a large garage. There was the Chrysler, a Volkswagen van, and beyond that his own Plymouth. Kavinsky stood by with a pistol at the ready while Goliath produced a pair of handcuffs and snapped one on Shaver's left wrist. After manhandling Shaver into the back of the Plymouth, he looped the chain around one of the steel bars supporting the headrest on the right front seat, then cuffed Shaver's other wrist, ensuring that he couldn't move from the rear of the car. Then his mouth was sealed with a strip of tape wrapped around his head so often that it would have to be cut away. Once this was accomplished, Kavinsky released Bogna, again standing by with his pistol while she was handcuffed in a similar fashion, even though she was in a drunken stupor and barely conscious.

Shaver thought that the smaller man was a particularly cautious little bastard and any hope of escape would only come when he was being transferred up front preliminary to the fatal plunge. They had to remove both the cuffs and the tape then, to make it look like an accident, and that would be his only and final chance, and he ought to have some sort of plan ready. But what could he possibly do against such hopeless odds?

Kavinsky satisfied himself that all was ready and then slid behind the wheel and signaled to Goliath to open the garage doors. The giant pushed a button on the wall and the doors moved up into the ceiling while he hurriedly got into the van. The Plymouth moved out first, nosing up a steep, winding driveway. The van followed close behind.

Samuel waited until he could no longer hear the motors of the departing vehicles. 'The drunken fool almost guessed the truth,' he said then.

'What does that matter?' Vostik asked. He took a small sampling sip of the Something Special. It was a good scotch, but he still preferred the bourbon, he decided.

O'Brien was in an unmarked police car headed for the Oak Street Bridge on the way to Vancouver International Airport. He was thinking that he should have got the ball rolling earlier on the missing-persons alert for Detective Sergeant Hardison. The whole day had been wasted and now nothing would be done tonight or tomorrow. Hardison's disappearance would be pushed aside while everyone concentrated on protecting a certain Alexei Kosygin.

'Is the ETA the same?' O'Brien asked his driver, suddenly aware that he hadn't been paying attention to the police radio.

'It's back to eight o'clock,' the driver reported. 'That's supposed to be definite, but it will change again, probably. What's the matter with the goddam Russkies? They're always bragging about their scientific achievements – and they can't even land a plane on schedule.'

'Headwinds,' O'Brien said absently, looking at his watch. It was just after seven and that meant it had been twelve hours since Hardison had failed to report for duty. Twelve hours was a long time for a police officer to go missing without some kind of word. By the looks of things, it wasn't a bender, after all. No matter how tanked he got, Hardison would have slept it off hours ago, and he knew enough to protect himself, didn't he? All that was required of him was a simple telephone call. One lousy minute to phone in and book off sick. Then he could go out and get drunk all over again. Nobody much gave a damn – just so long as he booked off.

'Before that, it was tailwinds,' the driver complained. 'They've gone full circle. Half a dozen changes and they're back right where they started. Eight o'clock ETA – and who gives a shit? You'd think someone was actually interested in the Commie bastard's precise moment of arrival.'

'The KGB is,' O'Brien said. 'They're precise in everything they do. One of the most efficient police organizations in the world . . .' He leaned forward and listened impatiently for a break in the rapid-fire transmissions on the police channel. 'Is that dispatcher ever going to shut up?'

'Are you kidding?' the driver laughed. He eased off the gas pedal in anticipation. 'If it's important, I'll pull in at a pay phone, Inspector. You'll get through a lot quicker that way.'

O'Brien shook his head no. They'd be at the airport in another five minutes and he'd make the telephone call from there. It wasn't all that vital – but he ought to discuss Hardison's disappearance with someone in authority at Vancouver Sub-division.

'Dispatch is putting on a real show,' the driver laughed. 'Now they're checking to see if everyone is in proper position. How's that for efficiency? Clogging up the airways for no goddam good reason.'

O'Brien didn't answer. He thought that he should have had a private chat with the Mounties long ago. It wouldn't have hurt if it was kept off the record. You could never tell with these things. The Mounties might be aware of some angle that figured in the case. Some small scrap of information that didn't mean anything unless it was put alongside the fact that a cop was missing. That was a wild longshot, but stranger things had happened, and you never knew unless you tried. Certainly the Mounties couldn't help as long as they were kept in the dark. They should have been informed long ago. It had been stupid to procrastinate.

'Listen to 'em, will you?' the driver said. 'What a bunch of blinking arseholes. If the KGB only knew, they'd never trust Kosygin to the Vancouver Police Force. If someone wanted to kill him, here's the ideal place.'

'That's enough of that,' O'Brien said.

Shaver had his bearings within a few moments after the Plymouth left the driveway of the house where he had been kept prisoner. The twisting waterfront highway with its steep rock cliffs and peeling arbutus was unique to the Lower Mainland. They could only be on the west shore and since the sea was to the left they were headed north toward Fisherman's Cove.

It didn't leave much time, Shaver thought. There were many places within the next few miles where an 'accident' could be staged with guaranteed results. He visualized the Plymouth ripping through a guardrail and arcing through space, the shattering impact as the car knifed into the water, the wild rush of air bubbles as it settled to the bottom.

Shaver thought there was no way to avoid it – he could already feel himself being relentlessly sucked to that watery grave – and then the car suddenly turned up a steep gravel road and his vision of death changed just as abruptly. The Plymouth hanging for a moment at the lip of a canyon and then dropping down, down, down. A bone-crushing crash. A searing whoosh of flame . . .

'It won't be long now,' Kavinsky said, as if reading his tortured thoughts. 'There's a new bridge under construction on the Upper Levels Highway. You're so stupid drunk, you're going to drive past the part where the bridge stops and empty space begins . . .' He glanced back over his shoulder. 'It won't be long. Just whatever number of seconds it takes to drop three hundred feet.'

Shaver ran that scene through his mind and felt himself

starting to get sick. He could see the detour barriers being knocked aside, the slab of concrete stretching out into a blue-black void, the edge drawing nearer and nearer . . .

'Think of how lucky you are,' Kavinsky laughed, shifting to a lower gear. 'If a misadventure verdict wasn't necessary – accidental death, possible suicide – you wouldn't be departing in such a quick, clean fashion. The colonel would have devised something unusual for you. Your agony would have been excruciating – and it would have gone on forever.'

Shaver wasn't listening. His stomach was churning and he could taste the bile at the back of his throat. He had still another vision of death and it was the worst of all. He was going to vomit and the tape was going to hold it in and he was going to choke to death on his own stinking wastes.

'Ever hit your thumb with a hammer?' Kavinsky asked, gunning into a curve. 'You know what that feels like. Imagine both thumbs and then your fingers. Imagine your balls.'

Shaver started thrashing convulsively. Twisting and turning, kicking out wildly, he got his bound feet onto the back seat, then up over Bogna, then against the roof. Using his handcuffed wrists as a fulcrum, he flung himself over the front seat, his knees pumping madly, his doubled-up boots a relentless battering ram.

Kavinsky was a split second too late reacting to the crazed assault. Everything seemed to go wrong at the same instant. He was trying to steer with one hand and get his pistol out with the other and he hit the brakes too hard and the car started to spin out of control. He slammed up against the windshield – helpless to defend himself against the vicious pounding – and watched strangely fascinated as the gravel was transformed into huge boulders. He felt the initial crash and was aware of the first cartwheel and then that was all. The Plymouth rolled twice more before coming to rest upside down against a massive fir tree.

Shaver's clawing fingers had hold of Kavinsky's coat even before the car stopped. He frantically tore at the material until he reached the right pocket and grabbed hold of the precious key. He unlocked his cuffs and then pulled Kavinsky's unconscious form closer to him along the roof of the car. He felt blindly for the pistol and found it just as Goliath reached the upturned vehicle and yanked open the door next to his head.

Don't think, Shaver told himself, and he stuck the pistol against the huge chest, pulling the trigger as he did so. There was an explosion and Goliath fell back with a strangely effeminate grunting sound. Shaver tried to finish him off with a second shot, but the angle was impossible from his upside-down position. Despite the terrible wound, Goliath managed to drag himself clear, clawing his way across the rocks. Could he live very long? Still pose a threat . . . ?

Don't think, Shaver told himself once more, and this time he grabbed Kavinsky by the throat and pressed the pistol against his temple, averting his own face from the mess that would splatter him when the second explosion came. He was starting to squeeze the trigger before he realized that he couldn't feel a pulse and that it wouldn't be necessary to dirty himself. His intended victim was already dead.

Shaver was barely aware of the rest of it. He seemed to be two persons and one was watching the other as if from a great distance. He saw himself pull Kavinsky's corpse closer, search the body for a pocketknife, use the knife to cut away the tape over his mouth and the rope tying his feet; he saw himself free Bogna and pull her from the wreck and start dragging her back up the hill toward the Volkswagen van; he watched more in resignation than alarm when the mortally wounded Goliath lurched into the van's headlights brandishing a rifle – and he smiled knowingly when he discovered that he had somehow lost the pistol and was forced to turn back and go crashing blindly into the forest.

O'Brien had intended to telephone as soon as he reached the airport terminal, but he got embroiled in a dispute over press coverage restrictions when he walked in the door, and it was twenty after seven when he finally got to a pay phone. By that time, Inspector McDermott was not available, being en route from his office to the airport, and O'Brien reluctantly agreed to talk to Sub-Inspector Benson. It had been his experience that one never got any satisfaction from Benson.

'What can I do you out of?' Benson asked by way of starters.

'I was after McDermott, actually,' O'Brien said.

'Sorry. He's not here.'

'I know,' O'Brien said. 'The switchboard told me. I'm calling from the airport.'

'That's where he's headed.'

'I know,' O'Brien said. 'They told me. But we may be too busy to talk then.'

'He'll be there soon enough.'

'This has nothing to do with Kosygin,' O'Brien said, becoming angry. He felt like someone had him by the seat of the pants and was running him out the door. 'One of my men has gone missing. Detective Sergeant Hardison.'

'So I see,' Benson said, his tone changing. He had detected the anger and was adjusting accordingly. 'I was just reading your missing-persons bulletin. Don't blame you for being worried. I'd be too if he was mine.'

'You've read the whole bulletin?'

'Sure,' Benson lied. He had read the first couple of paragraphs and put it aside. There were more important things afoot tonight.

'I was phoning to ask your special attention,' O'Brien said. 'You might have some ideas that haven't occurred to me. I've mentioned one case in particular that Hardison was working on. The chap involved has a minor record as a troublemaker. He might be known to your department.'

'I saw that,' Benson said, still lying. He thought he was being marvelously noncommittal.

'I don't trust these sex perverts,' O'Brien said.

'Who'd ever want to?' Benson agreed.

'Well,' O'Brien said, thinking that he was getting nowhere, as expected. He'd be further ahead to wait and talk to McDermott. 'Let me know if something comes to mind.'

'You've my word on that,' Benson promised, hanging up. He started to check his out basket for the missing-persons bulletin and then changed his mind. O'Brien would be talking to McDermott – McDermott could worry about it.

Benson thought that if he was going to volunteer for extra

work, he'd take on something interesting, such as that suspiciously tidy package presented by the disappearance of Corporal Shaver et al. That, now, was a missing-persons case that really did bear investigation, and he ought to look into it just as soon as possible. Benson thought about it for a while and promised himself he'd do something just as soon as they had Kosygin safely out of town. One had to remember priorities. First things first.

Shaver dragged Bogna down the mountain side, crashing into trees, stumbling over rocks, slipping on wet moss. He was oblivious to the pain of the cuts and bruises he was picking up in the wild scramble and barely conscious of Bogna's screams. He was a man possessed and he had only one thought – to reach a telephone.

He was plunging down blindly, able to see only a few yards ahead through the tangle of branches, but he knew he eventually had to come out onto Marine Drive, where he could flag down a motorist for help. If he stumbled upon a house, so much the better, but he wasn't going to waste time looking for one. The road was down there somewhere and there was a lot of local traffic and someone would stop soon enough. He'd lie in the goddam road if necessary.

They were going to make it, Shaver told himself, slashing wildly through the trees, and then Bogna fell and refused to get up. She let her body go limp and became a deadweight. She vowed she wouldn't take another step.

'Get up, damn you,' Shaver cursed, tugging at her viciously. 'You've got to keep going. You must.'

'No,' she gasped, her last reserves of strength gone. 'I can't . . .' She closed her eyes and surrendered to the strange euphoria suddenly sweeping her. 'Leave me.'

Shaver released her wrist and sagged down against a rotting windfall. It wasn't in him to carry her and he couldn't find the courage to go on alone. It would be pitch black soon and it might take a search party hours to locate her in this wretched tangle. What if she was badly hurt? So weak and exhausted that she couldn't hang on . . . ?

Shaver swore and wished that he wasn't so stupidly drunk. Somewhere along the line he'd lost the will to keep a clear head. The mirror-image clarity had been shattered and he couldn't trust the jumble of impressions swimming before his eyes. There probably was nothing wrong with Bogna. She had just got so tired that she'd fallen asleep. He could leave her and she'd be fine. Just fine . . .

Which was it? Shaver wondered. Was she hurt and dying or just tired and sleeping and why couldn't he tell the difference? His mind became fuzzier, the jumble of impressions fading away, becoming smaller, more distant, disappearing. Sleep, Shaver thought. Wonderful sleep. Wonderful, wonderful – sleep.

A dog barked and he opened his eyes and he wasn't sure what had happened or how much time had passed. He looked at his watch and saw that the crystal was smashed and the second hand wasn't working. He held it to his ear and couldn't hear any ticking. He looked back at the face of the watch. It had stopped at 7:52. He wondered how long ago that had been. A minute? An hour?

The dog barked again and Shaver staggered painfully to his feet. A dog meant a house and the house couldn't be far away. He could hear the dog barking very plainly. It was a loud, friendly, happy bark. It was somewhere just below him.

Shaver pulled Bogna over his shoulder and started down the mountain side once more. He kept to his feet for only a few steps before stumbling and falling. He got up again and made it a few steps farther the next time. He kept plunging down that way. Stumbling, falling, sliding. Dragging his burden.

The dog kept barking. But it seemed to be getting farther away.

The Chrysler was cutting across a field toward the landing pad on the north side of First Narrows when the helicopter with the fake Vancouver Police Department markings came clattering under Lions Gate Bridge. Colonel Vostik looked at his watch and smiled with approval. Split-second timing was crucial every step of the way – and the timing on this first step was perfect.

'Fat Boy, this is Teacher,' Vostik said, thumbing his radio transmitter button. 'Do you read me?'

The pilot's voice responded immediately. 'Teacher, this is Fat Boy. Loud and clear.'

'Come get your egg, Fat Boy,' Vostik said.

'Roger,' the pilot said.

The Chrysler reached the edge of the landing pad at the same instant the chopper touched down. Henke, moving in a daze, rigged with a strange-looking harness, was pulled from the back seat of the car and pushed up into the aircraft. Samuel swung up aboard with him. Vostik remained behind.

The pilot looked at his watch and made a circle with the thumb and forefinger of his right hand. Vostik smiled and waved and ran back to the car. The chopper lifted off and headed back out over the water.

'Fat Boy, this is Teacher,' Vostik transmitted from the Chrysler. 'Listen to Eagle Eye. Rotsa ruck.'

'Thank you, Teacher,' the pilot said.

Vostik smiled again and sat listening to the subsequent transmissions as the chopper flew back under Lions Gate Bridge to its holding position in English Bay.

'Fat Boy, this is Eagle Eye. Do you read me?'

'Eagle Eye, this is Fat Boy. Loud and clear.'

'Good news, Fat Boy. Big Daddy will soon be on his way. We're estimating half an hour. We'll keep you posted and see you then.'

'Right on.'

Right on, Vostik agreed, looking at his watch. He started the Chrysler and swung across the landing pad and headed for the Park Royal shopping center to rendezvous with the Volkswagen van.

Right on, Samuel thought, busy fastening the plastic explosives to the harness fitted to Henke, who sat stupefied and unaware of what was happening or why.

Sixteen

Shaver couldn't believe it had happened. One moment he had been hopelessly lost in a dense black forest. The next he was standing in the middle of a neatly manicured yard. It was as if a miracle had occurred — and all that had been required was for him to blunder through one more thicket.

Praise God, Shaver thought, starting for the low, dark shadow of a house. He had been ready to give up and some inner voice had urged him on. He had been prepared to throw himself down in surrender and some mysterious force he had never experienced before had insisted that he push on.

Shaver staggered across the lawn and lurched down a short run of flagstone steps and was suddenly hit by a blinding light. At the same moment a dog started barking in a wild frenzy as it tore loose from restraint.

A harsh command followed: 'Don't move!'

Shaver froze. He closed his eyes against the light and raised his arms to protect himself from the dog's attack. He felt Bogna slip off his shoulder and fall to the ground behind him and he thought that he also had to save her from the dog. He didn't know what else to do so he lowered himself until he was sitting cross-legged on her head.

Now a question came from the shadows: 'What the dickens . . . ?' The spotlight blinked off and more subdued lighting bathed the yard. Shaver saw that the wild beast about to tear out his throat was actually a cocker spaniel with its head stuck through the bottom of a plastic pail. Its owner, a stumpy old man with a shock of white hair, hurried down the back stairs of the house, more concerned now with the dog than his battered visitors. The animal was barking furiously and running around in an ever-widening circle that would soon bring it into collision with the house.

'You planning to hatch that gal?' the old man asked Shaver, getting himself set in the cocker's path. The animal came by and he reached out with surprising agility to grab hold of the trailing leash.

'Help,' Shaver said weakly, easing himself off Bogna. 'Need help . . .' He rose unsteadily to his feet. 'Please.'

The old man tucked the squirming dog under his left arm and then reached out to shake hands. 'The name's MacDougall and this varmint here is Bugle MacDougall. The Doc put his head in the pail. Stops him from eating out his stitches.'

'Emergency,' Shaver said. 'Must phone . . .' He pulled his hand away. 'Got to call police.'

'An accident, huh?' the old man said. 'That's what happened to Bugle. Chased a cat onto the road.' He bent down to examine Bogna. 'Where'd it happen? Back up the ridge?'

'Got to call police . . .'

'I'd think twice about that,' the old man said. He pushed back an eyelid and satisfied himself that Bogna was alive. Then he took hold of her wrist to check her pulse. 'Anybody else involved?'

'Please.'

'Suit yourself,' the old man said, smelling Bogna's breath. 'But what makes you think you're sober enough to dial?'

'Then you do it,' Shaver told him, pulling out his wallet. 'See that badge? I'm police. Must phone Kosygin.'

'Kosygin?' the old man asked, some real interest aroused at last. 'What have you got to do with him?'

'Assass . . .' Shaver said hopelessly. 'Assass . . .' He tried to put the wallet back and couldn't find his pocket. 'Killers. Must stop killers.'

The old man hesitated only a moment before making up his mind. The badge looked real enough and the newspaper was full of Kosygin's impending visit. There would be time later for questions, and only good, not harm, could result from helping a man, no matter how unlikely the situation.

'Why stand around then?' he demanded. He tied up the dog and led Shaver into the house and dialed Vancouver

Sub-division for him. He made sure of the connection and then went back outside to get Bogna.

'This is an emergency,' Shaver babbled into the phone. 'Need the senior officer on duty. Threat against Kosygin ...' He took a deep breath and tried to calm himself. 'Hurry.'

'Who is this calling, please?' a thin voice piped.

'Never mind, damn you,' Shaver yelled. 'Put me through to a senior officer. McDermott there? Benson?'

'Sub-Inspector Benson is on duty, but his line is busy at the moment, I'm afraid,' the young constable on the switchboard answered. 'Could I have your name, please?'

'Shaver,' Shaver screamed. 'Corporal Shaver. You stupid son of a bitch. Didn't you hear me? Kosygin is going to be killed ...'

'I can hear you.'

'Then break into the call. Put me through to Benson.'

'I'll need more information before doing that,' the constable said. He flipped through the charge sheets on the clipboard at his elbow and found the one he wanted. Corporal Timothy Shaver, charged with assault causing bodily harm, and, by the sound of him, the corporal also could be arrested for drunkenness.

'Give me the radio room then,' Shaver ordered, barely able to speak.

'Not in your condition,' the young constable told him.

'You fool,' Shaver raged. 'You goddam pipsqueak ...' There was a click and then the buzzing sound indicating that his call had been placed on hold. He slumped down in a chair and sat listening to the buzz and cursing the world's most overrated police force. He could picture the youth with his peach fuzz and pimples. Fresh out of high school – if indeed he ever finished – and that's why he was working the phones on this night of all nights. The Mounties have an image to worry about and they like to keep the recruits out of sight until they're at least of drinking age.

The old man struggled into the house with Bogna. 'Problems?'

Shaver nodded dully and was about to hang up when the young constable came on the phone again. 'Sub-Inspector Benson's line is still busy.'

'Break in!' Shaver yelled, but it was too late. He was already back on hold.

Benson got himself positioned in front of the small television set he had taken from McDermott's office. If he knew the inspector, the vain bastard would be wanting to know how he looked on the telly, and he should have something factual to report along with the bullshit. It would help to recount something that actually happened on the flickering screen, such as McDermott throwing his precious body atop a sputtering bomb, ha, ha.

Benson smiled and edged closer to the set. Behind him, the phone he had left off the hook buzzed faintly, drowned out by the roar of the jet aircraft he was watching.

In another part of sub-division headquarters, the young constable on the switchboard was talking to the chief operator at the telephone company, arranging to have Shaver's call traced. This could earn him a commendation, he thought. The assault charge wasn't bad enough. Now the corporal was drunk and making crank calls. The sooner he was nabbed, the better for the force, and the telephone company would have him pinpointed in another minute or so.

The youth put the operator on hold and switched briefly to Shaver. 'Sub-Inspector Benson's line is still busy.'

'Would it help if I talked for you?' the old man asked. He dragged Bogna to a sofa and got her stretched out on it and then sat down himself, out of breath.

'No,' Shaver said. He thought that it would just complicate matters if he hung up and had the old man call back with the same story. The punk on the switchboard still wouldn't break in on Benson. Nor was there any use trying to explain the situation to the city police. It was essential that he reach someone who knew him and who would accept his story without asking a lot of stupid questions. There simply wasn't time for explanations.

'Your lady friend's okay,' the old man said. 'Far as I can tell, she's just drunk, is all. Smells like a distillery.' He shook his head and decided not to press it until the crisis was resolved. 'I've got some coffee I could warm up. Interested?'

'Please,' Shaver said. He looked up from the phone, thinking that he should show he was grateful for the assistance, and for the first time he became aware of the television set in the corner of the living room, the picture on but the sound turned off. There was a shot of an airliner on the screen, turning off the runway after landing, and when the camera zoomed in for a close-up he could see the Russian markings. Shaver stared at the picture and then it finally penetrated his muddled brain that he didn't know what time it was and that Kosygin might have arrived hours ago and could be safe in bed at the Hotel Vancouver by now.

'That's Kosygin, all right,' the old man said, noticing Shaver's look. He crossed to the television and turned up the volume. 'This is live coverage of his arrival.'

'Live?' Shaver echoed. 'He's arriving now?'

The old man nodded and pulled out his pocketwatch. 'Eight o'clock on the button.'

Shaver broke his connection and held out the phone. 'Get the airport. Page a police officer. Any police officer in the main terminal.'

'You know the number?'

'The operator. Tell her it's an emergency. Life or death . . .'

The old man again hesitated only briefly. He thought he'd get a few months in jail at most for a crank call and it was an experience he had missed so far. Besides, drunk or not, the bloke did have a badge. 'All right.'

Shaver stood staring at the television as the call was put through. He could remember coming up the stairs in the house where he had been kept drugged. Vostik had been circling the living room, pretending that he was an airplane, and he had plunged into the sofa, making the noise of a loud explosion. Shaver thought that this could happen any moment now on the screen. A small aircraft packed with explosives could dive into view just as Kosygin started down the ramp.

'They're paging now,' the old man said, offering the phone.

'You talk to them,' Shaver ordered. 'I'm too drunk . . .' He saw the old man's expression and hastened to reassure him.

'I'll talk to Inspector McDermott if you can get him. My boss. Knows me.'

'And if I can't get McDermott?'

Shaver saw that the old man was still doubtful and he knew that the police officer who answered the page would have the same expression. Nor was there much doubt as to what he'd say. *Sure, sure, Mac. There's a kamikaze pilot coming in right now. He's gonna go boom and we're all gonna fall down dead. Thanks for the warning – and make the next drink on me.*

'Better insist on McDermott,' Shaver said, watching the television expectantly. The ramp was being pushed up against the Russian aircraft. Security guards were moving into position.

'Hello?' the old man said into the phone. 'Is this a police officer? I've got an emergency call for Inspector McDermott.'

'The RCMP,' Shaver added. The door of the aircraft was swinging open.

'He's with the RCMP,' the old man said dutifully.

'Skip it,' Shaver said, reaching for the phone. There were more security men in the picture now. One of them was McDermott and he was too far from the phone. 'Hello. Who's this?'

'Constable Perkins.'

'City Police?'

'Yes. I answered a page for a police officer.'

'Listen,' Shaver said, speaking as distinctly as possible. 'My name's Shaver. With the RCMP. Kosygin's in danger.'

'Oh? What kind?'

'Not sure,' Shaver said. 'Bomb threat, probably. Watch for light aircraft. Coming in any moment. It'll either drop a bomb or crash.'

'What bar are you calling from?'

'If you don't believe me, get McDermott,' Shaver begged. 'Inspector McDermott. He's out there at the plane. I can see him on television ...' He stopped because he was slurring hopelessly. 'McDermott. Knows me. Get him.'

'Sure,' he was told, and the phone went dead.

Vostik swung the Chrysler off the Marine Drive and headed up the gravel road leading to the construction work on the Upper Levels Highway. He had waited five minutes past the appointed time for the Volkswagen van to rendezvous at Park Royal. When it hadn't shown up by then, he had set out to investigate, and he knew now – since he hadn't met the van on the road – that some disaster had struck.

If the fools had bungled, he'd kill them, Vostik vowed. What could be more simple than to dispose of a staggering drunk and an unconscious woman? Only the worst kind of idiots could botch that.

The Chrysler rounded a corner and Vostik felt his heart drop out of him. The Volkswagen van was parked in the middle of the road with its headlights aimed into a rocky gully. At the bottom, barely visible at the outer perimeter of the swath of light, Shaver's upturned Plymouth was a mechanical monster gone berserk, the rear wheels spinning and the motor racing wildly.

The fools, Vostik thought. The stupid, demented, bungling fools. He pulled over and slipped out on the passenger's side and dropped down into the ditch.

He carefully worked his way forward, pistol drawn, prepared for any eventuality, and then made a final rush that put the van between himself and the Plymouth. The racing motor warned him that he had to be careful. Kavinsky, the driver, could have been killed or knocked unconscious in the crash, but why hadn't Goliath turned it off. One explanation was that the giant had slipped and fallen in a mad rush to the wreck. But there were other possibilities . . .

Vostik wondered if the impossible had actually happened. What if both Kavinsky and Goliath were dead? What if Shaver had somehow managed to free himself?

If so, Shaver could be armed, hiding, waiting. This could be a trap. Death could be lurking in those dark shadows.

So many tactical questions – and no time to resolve them.

Vostik lunged out of the ditch and crossed the road in a low crouch. He zigzagged down the gully and flung himself to the ground when he was within twenty yards of the Plymouth. From there he could see that it was empty except for Kavinsky's body.

So Shaver had escaped and the woman with him? But where had he gone and why hadn't he taken the van? Because he was too drunk to drive? – or because Goliath had chased him into the forest?

If there was a God, he'd be praying now, Vostik thought. For Goliath to catch them in time. To kill them before they reached help ...

If You exist, make it happen, please, Vostik whispered, slithering across the rocks to the Plymouth. He reached under the crumpled hood and ripped off the distributor cap. The roar of the motor stopped and he was momentarily deaf in the silence that followed and then he heard a rock rattle behind him.

So it was a trap? Vostik whirled and fired and the slug ripped point blank into Goliath's face. The giant took a last step – his mouth blowing a bubble of blood – and then pitched forward like a felled tree.

Vostik's skin was crawling as he backed away. He saw more than just the giant's corpse. He also saw his own. That one fearful fear-driven bullet had destroyed everything. With no one to point the way, there was no chance of catching Shaver, and even if the corporal was too drunk to save Kosygin, he'd sober up eventually and reveal that the KGB did the job.

The colonel raised the pistol to his shaved skull. The price of failure was death and he preferred that he be his own executioner. His finger started to squeeze the trigger and then it occurred to him that there was a way of foiling Shaver. Who would believe the corporal's story if nothing happened to Kosygin?

Vostik started scrambling madly up the hill. He had to call off the operation. He had to save Kosygin.

But did he have time ... ?

Seventeen

Shaver sat gulping down black coffee as he watched the live television coverage of Kosygin's arrival. The Russian leader had deplaned without incident, nothing untoward had occurred during the brief welcoming ceremony on the tarmac, and now he was moving through the crowd inside the terminal and still there was no sign of trouble. Yet surely it must come soon?

'More?' the old man asked, refilling his cup without waiting for a reply.

'Please,' Shaver said, intent on the screen. The phone was forgotten now. Time had run out and there was no way he could stop the inevitable.

'Looks like you were wrong,' the old man said suspiciously.

'We'll soon see,' Shaver said. He decided that the aircraft theory must be wrong and that a sniper would do the job. There'd be a crucial moment when Kosygin left the terminal to get into his limousine. He'd be out in the open again – and an expert marksman could hit him from a couple hundred yards.

'If they were going to do it, they'd have done it on the tarmac, wouldn't they?' the old man demanded. 'They had all kinds of time then.'

'You'd think so,' Shaver admitted, but he told himself that it would be difficult to position a sniper on the runway side of the terminal. There were better hiding places in front of the building.

'I know so,' the old man grumbled.

Shaver ignored him and edged closer to the screen. Kosygin was passing through the front door of the terminal, smiling and waving. He was crossing the sidewalk to the waiting limousine. The crowd was pressing forward and jostling the police. Now a news cameraman lost his footing in the rush. He swung around awkwardly, trying to keep his balance and still hold the camera, and it was suddenly thrust into the center of the picture, the sole focus of attention.

'That's it!' Shaver yelled. He sat frozen until Kosygin's limousine moved out of range and then told himself that he had two choices. He could keep trying with the phone, hoping to reach someone somewhere who wouldn't dismiss him as a blubbering drunk, or he could try to intercept the motorcade, stopping the Russian leader from reaching the Hotel Vancouver.

'What do you mean?' the old man asked.

'There's no time to explain,' Shaver said. 'I've got to get out of here. Do you have a car?'

'Yes, but if you're thinking of borrowing it, think again. You're still too drunk to drive.'

Shaver pushed to his feet. 'I haven't time to argue . . .'

The old man made the mistake of glancing at the bureau top where he'd left the keys. 'I'll take you wherever you want.'

'No,' Shaver told him. 'That wouldn't be fast enough, and I want you here, phoning the police. Tell them Kosygin is a dead man if he goes to the Hotel Vancouver.'

'They won't believe me.'

'That's the trouble,' Shaver said, snatching up the keys. 'They won't believe me either. So I've got to do it this way.'

Vostik kept carefully under the speed limit as he drove back along Marine Drive toward Park Royal. He didn't dare take the chance of being stopped by a police cruiser. Not with a corpse in the back seat and another in the trunk.

Besides, Vostik thought, monitoring the city police radio channel, there was plenty of time now. Kosygin's motorcade was just crossing the Oak Street Bridge. It would be another twenty minutes before it reached the Hotel Vancouver. Long before that – in less than five minutes – the Chrysler would be back within transmitting range of the helicopter.

Vostik thought that he had accomplished a miracle under the circumstances. He had hidden the van and cleaned out the wrecked Plymouth – taken the handcuffs and pieces of tape and rope Shaver had left discarded inside – so that there was nothing at the crash scene to substantiate Shaver's story. On the contrary, the authorities might be inclined to think that he had crashed the car, then made up a wild tale to protect himself.

Nor was the Polack slut a problem. She had been barely conscious during that unfortunate session when he had boasted too freely before Shaver. She had heard nothing of the KGB aspect and what little she could tell would make it appear that she was lying to protect her lover.

But the real reason that Shaver's story would be dismissed as poppycock was that nothing – absolutely nothing – was going to happen to Kosygin. The Chrysler's transmitter would soon be in range. Just a few more minutes . . .

Vostik heard the wild honking and looked in the rear view mirror and pulled over just in time. An old Dodge sedan, swerving wildly, the driver barely in control, flashed by him at breakneck speed.

The colonel stared after it in disbelief. Had that been Shaver at the wheel?

The devil saves me, Vostik thought, slamming down on the accelerator. Shaver obviously hadn't informed the authorities of the threat against Kosygin. If he had, the police radio dispatcher would be going crazy by now, not checking the motorcade's progress in a routine fashion. Perhaps Shaver was too drunk to telephone. Or had been dismissed as a crank. Or was stupidly intent on some sort of personal intervention.

Vostik grinned and told himself that it didn't matter. If he could catch the drunken idiot – and catch him he would – the operation was going ahead. Kosygin's stay of execution had just been canceled.

McDermott listened in growing bewilderment and disbelief as Benson breathlessly recounted Shaver's latest exploits. Drunk in a stolen car . . . racing madly toward the Hotel Vancouver . . . babbling about an assassination attempt against Kosygin.

'Did he say how?' McDermott asked, thankful that Benson

had chosen the relative privacy of the radio-telephone.

'No,' Benson said. 'The old man says Shaver wasn't clear on that. First he claimed it was going to be a bomb dropped from an aircraft, but then he changed his mind when nothing happened. You've got the sum total of his departing message: "Tell them Kosygin is a dead man if he goes to the hotel."'

McDermott shook his head despairingly. 'It sounds like our corporal has bought the nut farm. What do you think?'

'I don't know,' Benson confessed. 'Ordinarily, I'd say he was drunk, that's all, and forget it. But the other stuff worries me. Special Branch. Henke ...' His voice faded. 'I don't know.'

Nor I, McDermott decided, thinking that this was a fine fucking mess. He couldn't divert the motorcade on the sayso of a drunken corporal, and he couldn't let the warning go unheeded, either. He had to figure some way of protecting his ass.

'Buy me some time,' McDermott said at last. 'I want to talk to Shaver at the hotel before Kosygin arrives. Contact the city police dispatcher and tell him to slow this parade to thirty miles per hour – and to make sure Shaver has a free run into town.'

'The superintendent will have a shit fit.'

'Refer him to me if there are any questions. I'll be conveniently out of radio contact.'

'What about when Shaver reaches the hotel? Do you want him taken into custody then?'

'Yes. Grab him and hold him for me. We'll meet in the lobby. Georgia Street entrance.'

'Right. Anything else?'

'Cross your fingers,' McDermott suggested. He hung up the radio-telephone and switched on his siren and pulled out of position in the motorcade. If the dispatcher reduced its speed to thirty, he'd beat it to the hotel by a good five minutes, he thought. That would give him time to have Kosygin diverted if necessary. But Shaver had to be awfully convincing for him to do that. Goddam convincing.

As McDermott swept past the lead car, RCMP Superintendent Sibley, the security chief assigned to Kosygin from

Ottawa, spoke sharply to his driver. 'Who in the hell is that?'

'Inspector McDermott, sir.'

Sibley reached for the radio. 'Oh? He'd better have a good explanation.'

'This is a city police unit,' the driver reminded Sibley. 'The inspector's on a different radio frequency. But the city dispatcher can relay a message through the Sub-division radio room.'

'It's not important,' Sibley said, coloring slightly. He replaced the microphone and turned and smiled reassuringly to the KGB officers sitting in the back seat of the cruiser. They stared back at him impassively.

A piss-poor show, Sibley thought. All the cars in the motorcade ought to be on the same frequency. He wouldn't let that happen again – and he'd also be chewing McDermott at the first opportunity.

Farther back in the motorcade, O'Brien was thinking that he had lost still another chance to talk to McDermott, whom he had missed in the confusion at the airport. But it really didn't matter. Benson had all the details.

If there was any justice in the world, Shaver would be a dead man by now, Vostik decided. The stolen Dodge was only four cars ahead of him on the west-shore approach to Lions Gate Bridge. Traffic was moving at a walking pace as three lanes of converging vehicles jockeyed for position on the bridge's one city-bound lane.

Vostik could have killed Shaver at least a dozen times since catching up to him at the bridge. All he had to do was get out of his car and run up alongside the Dodge. Shaver had his window down and his head out cursing the driver ahead of him. He'd be aware of nothing until he felt the pistol at the base of his skull – and then it would be too late.

But the problem, of course, was that this meant abandoning the Chrysler, which would then be trapped in the jam-up behind the Dodge. Vostik didn't dare leave the car with its telltale communications system and its two KGB corpses. He could destroy it where it stood – he had prepared for such a necessity – but this was a last resort and the wrong place for it. He couldn't be sure of escaping.

Vostik swore in frustration and tuned down the city police radio so that he could monitor the transmissions between the lookout at the Hotel Vancouver and the helicopter over English Bay.

'Fat Boy, this is Eagle Eye,' the lookout was saying. 'We're now estimating Big Daddy in fifteen minutes. Will you start your final run, please?'

'Roger, Eagle Eye,' the pilot responded. 'We read you as estimating fifteen minutes – and we're starting our final run.'

One more reason for sticking with the Chrysler, Vostik thought. As long as he stayed, his options remained open, permitting him to stop the operation right up until the final seconds. Leaving the radio meant that the operation went ahead regardless.

Vostik told himself that he had no choice but to be patient. They'd be across the bridge soon, and if he couldn't overtake Shaver on the causeway through Stanley Park, there were ten long blocks between the park and the hotel. He had the faster car and Shaver was drunk. How could he fail?

Benson hung up on the city police radio dispatcher and got out his handkerchief. The dispatcher had been dubious, but he had agreed to co-operate, thank God. Kosygin's motorcade would be slowed. Shaver was to get a clear run.

Now came the worst part, Benson thought. The waiting for the thing to be over and done with. He had a foreboding of disaster and almost wished that he was in McDermott's place. For McDermott, racing the clock, time would fly – but it would only crawl for clock-watchers.

Benson wiped his face with his handkerchief and turned up the volume of the city broadcast monitor. He noted with satisfaction that the dispatcher was already relaying the request to slow Kosygin's motorcade. The sergeant leading the motorcade motorcycle escort responded affirmatively but the order was challenged a moment later.

'By whose authority?' someone demanded, and Benson stiffened when he recognized the voice. It was Superintendent Sibley, the security chief sent out from Ottawa, and Benson had thought that he'd be going on ahead in the police helicopter, not riding with the motorcade.

'Vancouver Sub-division, sir,' the dispatcher replied. 'Requested by Inspector McDermott and relayed by the Sub-Inspector Benson.'

'Inspector McDermott is not in charge of this motorcade,' Sibley said stiffly.

'Yessir. Do you wish to cancel, sir?'

'What reason did McDermott give?' Sibley asked.

'None, sir,' the dispatcher said, his voice strained now. 'It was Sub-Inspector Benson who relayed the request. He assured me it was important . . .'

Sibley cut in on him. 'Ask Sub-division radio room to contact McDermott.'

'Yessir.'

Now O'Brien cut in. 'That was McDermott who left the motorcade, Superintendent.'

'I realize that,' Sibley said, becoming angry, 'and I want to know why he ran off, and I want to know why he's cut our speed, goddam it.'

'Yessir,' the dispatcher repeated.

Benson was reminded that he had lied to O'Brien when the city homicide chief telephoned about his missing-persons bulletin. Reading it would give him something to do. It would be better than sitting and waiting.

Shaver had the old Dodge wound up to its top speed, sixty miles an hour, as he flashed out of Stanley Park onto Georgia Street, barely beating a red light. He heard a loud crashing noise behind him and looked back to see a Cortina sedan spinning in the intersection and a familiar black Chrysler lurching toward the sidewalk. Vostik?

Shaver braked to avoid colliding with the cars in front of him, which were slowing now in anticipation of the next signal light, and when he looked again he saw death looming in confirmation. Vostik had regained control of the Chrysler and was driving along the sidewalk opposite him. The colonel had his window rolled down and was trying to steer with his stump while aiming a pistol.

The first slug tore through the Dodge's windshield before

Shaver could react, and then he instinctively chose the only escape route open to him. He pressed down on the gas and swung out over the center strip into the path of oncoming traffic as two more bullets shattered the rear window. A Volkswagen hit the Dodge head-on in the first lane, caving in the passenger's side, but Shaver managed to keep moving, getting across the second lane with only a side swipe from a light Datsun truck. He ran up onto the sidewalk and started honking wildly to clear it of pedestrians.

On the far sidewalk, Vostik drove to the next intersection, then cut back onto the road, gradually working his way into the left lane. He knew he could no longer delay making his kill. Police sirens would be wailing any moment now.

Vostik searched desperately for a break in the oncoming traffic while another part of his mind listened to the transmissions between the lookout and the helicopter pilot.

'Fat Boy, this is Eagle Eye. We're estimating ten minutes. Could we have your position, please?'

'Eagle Eye, this is Fat Boy. We're off Third Beach and holding.'

'Hold until advised, Fat Boy.'

'Roger, Eagle Eye. We read you as holding until advised.'

It had to be now, Vostik thought. He gritted his teeth and swung left into the first opening he saw and almost made it to the curb when a taxi seemed to appear from nowhere. There was a grinding crash and the Chrysler spun around violently and slammed into a steel light standard.

Vostik was stunned but very much aware of his situation. The ignition was still on but the light on his transmitter had blinked out. That meant the battery had been disconnected – and that radio contact with the lookout was broken.

Eighteen

On the top floor of the Hotel Vancouver, in a room on the Burrard Street side, overlooking the motor entrance, the KGB agent directing the helicopter's flight peered cautiously through the venetian blinds. 'Fat Boy, this is Eagle Eye,' he said, speaking into his throat mike. 'We're estimating eight minutes. Start your final run, please.'

The helicopter pilot's answer knifed through the static in his earphones: 'Eagle Eye, this is Fat Boy. We read you as estimating eight minutes – and we're starting our final run.'

'Roger, thank you,' the agent said. He adjusted the blind so that he had a better view of Mueller, the amateur photographer, who was sitting cross-legged atop a truck in the parking lot on the opposite side of the street, checking the zoom lens on his Canon movie camera.

Everything was proceeding perfectly, the agent thought. He was getting a block-by-block report on the motorcade's progress, the helicopter was right on schedule, no one was paying any attention to the photographer, and even the colonel was co-operating by remaining off the air. It was amazing that something this complicated should go so smoothly – and especially that the colonel should keep his mouth shut.

The agent adjusted the blind to its former angle and wondered who or what had wrought such a remarkable and wondrous circumstance. If anything could upset the delicate timetable at this stage, it was the colonel with some totally irrelevant comment, blocking out a crucial transmission. But there hadn't been a peep out of him since he had put Henke aboard the helicopter at First Narrows – and that had been how long ago?

The agent's thoughts were interrupted by a radio message.

'Eagle Eye, this is Snooper. Twenty-fifth and Oak. Estimating seven minutes.'

'Roger, Snooper,' the agent said, forgetting about Vostik. Everything was going so smoothly. Why worry about how long the colonel had remained off the air? That wasn't a problem. It was a blessing.

Vostik reached for the glove compartment with a shaking hand. He withdrew six small silver canisters and stuffed them into his coat pocket and stumbled out of the wrecked Chrysler. While bystanders stared at him dumbly, he unlocked the trunk, pulled the timing mechanisms on two of the canisters, threw them inside with Kavinsky's corpse and then slammed the trunk lid shut. He tossed two more canisters in the back seat with Goliath and the last two up front just as a terrible whooshing sound exploded inside the trunk. By the time he had backed out into the middle of the street, the same terrible whoosh had flared twice more, in the front and the back of the car, and it was burning with an incredibly hot white heat. Witnesses were screaming and running for their lives even before the gas tank erupted in an orange fireball that sent a tower of black smoke tumbling skyward.

The colonel joined the mad scramble, dodging wildly among abandoned vehicles, until he reached the next intersection, where traffic was still moving. He pulled open the door of an Austin sedan that was slowly rounding the corner and slid in beside the driver. The man looked at him apprehensively. 'What happened back there?'

'A small accident,' Vostik said, screwing a silencer into his pistols. 'Two of my friends are being incinerated. There'll be nothing left to identify. Only a handful of ashes.'

'Hey,' the man said, staring at the pistol.

'Hey what?' Vostik asked. He squeezed off two shots and caught the wheel with his stump and steered into the curb.

Half a block ahead, on the opposite side of the street, Shaver was still driving crazily along the sidewalk, bounding off a fire hydrant, knocking over a postal box.

Vostik changed places with his victim and set off in

dogged pursuit. He fervently wished that he could do something more than simply kill Shaver. Mere death was too good for someone so impossibly obstinate.

Benson wondered why so much fuss was being made for nothing in the supposed disappearance of Detective Sergeant Hardison. Inspector O'Brien must love the bloke as a son. Hardison's description went on forever. Then a list of the criminals who might want a go at him. And another list of his current cases and ...

The name hit Benson like a kick in the face. HENKE, Rudolph Ivor.

'Son of a bitch,' Benson said softly. This couldn't be mere coincidence. He pushed up from his desk and ran for the radio room.

Shaver abandoned the Dodge and plunged into the middle of Georgia Street. He was near the downtown core now, less than two blocks from the hotel, and it was too dangerous to continue driving on the sidewalk. If he kept that up, he was going to kill someone for sure, or worse still, somebody was going to kill him. Only the wildest luck had got him this far without a police officer cutting him down like a mad dog.

He didn't want to risk that – not when he was this close to his goal – and he also wanted to make a relatively dignified arrival at the hotel. If he arrived drunk in a bullet-riddled wreck, he might be summarily whisked away to a jail cell by some thick-headed constable who believed in the paddy wagon first and questions later. Better that he simply arrive drunk.

That alone was bad enough, Shaver thought. Time was running out – every second was going to count – and the first police officer he encountered would probably seal Kosygin's fate one way or the other. It had to be someone in authority who knew him well enough to grant a fair hearing despite his condition. Otherwise ...

Shaver glanced back over his shoulder at the black smoke billowing skyward. With luck, that was the Chrysler, he thought, and Vostik was in it. There was no indication of the car following him any longer. No sign of the colonel.

Could he be that fortunate? Shaver wondered. Or was Vostik still dogging his footsteps? Was he taking aim with his pistol even now?

Shaver shut his mind to his fears and put on an extra burst of speed. He pounded desperately down the center line of the street, heedless of the cars brushing against him, the drivers yelling, the Austin sedan inching ever closer. Now there was only a block left to go. Now only half a block.

McDermott thought he'd go crazy if he heard one more call saying Superintendent Sibley demanded an explanation for the slowing of Kosygin's motorcade. He reached forward and switched off his radio.

As he did so, he heard someone other than the Sub-division dispatcher start to speak, and the voice seemed strangely excited and high-pitched. Like old lady Benson when someone shoved a hand up his skirt.

McDermott smiled and decided that he was imagining things. He left the radio off and concentrated on his driving. He'd be at the hotel soon, and he'd have a certain corporal by the throat, and he'd have an explanation for all this bloody nonsense.

Vostik stopped the Austin and rested on the open door to steady his aim. He fired once and missed and then fired once more and saw Shaver stumble and fall.

It was done! Vostik exulted. The bastard was down. All that remained was to finish him off. One more slug at close range. The coup de grâce.

Shaver took his hand away from his thigh and saw that it was covered with blood. He couldn't understand it – why hadn't he heard a shot? – and then he looked up and saw Vostik approaching. The colonel was walking very stiffly, almost like a soldier on parade, and he had his right arm held down at his side, the pistol and its silencer pointed at the pavement.

I'm dead, Shaver thought. He got ready to accept the next bullet before he realized that the truck next to him had stopped and that the driver was turning down his window.

'Get going, for Christ's sake,' Shaver screamed, rolling under the truck. He grabbed hold of the undercarriage and pulled himself up and stiffened his body.

The driver took one look at Vostik and then the truck roared forward.

Shaver stayed with it for only a few seconds. By then both shoes had been torn off and he couldn't bear the pain of being dragged on his heels. He let go and waited for the truck's rear wheels to slip by and then started rolling for the curb. He had made about six turns – his arms wrapped around his head for protection – when he realized there was something wrong. He should have reached the curb long ago. Where was it?

Shaver lowered his arms and saw that the truck had dragged him out into the middle of the intersection before he had let go. He was rolling up the middle of Burrard Street in full view of the crowd that had gathered at the hotel to wait for Kosygin's arrival.

The motorcycle officer on point duty at the intersection left the traffic signal control box and ran out into the street with his revolver drawn. He grabbed Shaver by the scruff of the neck and pulled him to his feet and marched him back to the sidewalk in front of the hotel. Besides the laughter, there were loud boos from the crowd, which included a number of anti-Russian demonstrators.

The officer decided that it would be best if he took his prisoner inside the hotel. Another constable moved in to help but was told to take over the signal light control instead. There'd be an order soon to halt all traffic crossing Burrard.

'I'm RCMP!' Shaver kept shouting, vainly trying to struggle free.

'Sure, sure,' the motorcycle officer said, marching him across the lobby with his arm twisted behind his back.

'My wallet,' Shaver cried. 'Identification . . .' He screamed in pain as his arm was twisted higher. 'You stupid bastard. I'm RCMP.'

'Sure, sure,' the motorcycle officer repeated. He kept the pressure on Shaver's arm until they were inside an assistant manager's officer that had been set aside for police use. Then he released his grip and pushed Shaver against the wall. 'Now. Are you going to submit to the cuffs – or would you like a few lumps first?'

Shaver bounced off the wall like a prize fighter coming off the ropes. His left fist slammed into his captor's face and sent him reeling across the room. He caught him in the face again with an even harder blow as he slumped dazedly into a chair. Then he finished him off with a vicious judo chop to the back of the neck as he slumped to the floor.

'What the hell?'

Shaver swung around to see another police officer standing dumbfounded in the doorway. He had a rifle slung over his shoulder and was trying to get it into firing position.

There was no use trying to explain, Shaver thought. He lashed out with his murderous left and the newcomer was soon sprawled on the floor beside his fellow officer.

Shaver was going to give up – he could see the entire city police force piled up like cordwood while he vainly searched for someone to listen to him – and then the high-powered rifle gave him an idea. If he could get upstairs in the hotel . . . if he could start firing into the street . . .

If he did that, they'd damn well divert Kosygin's motorcade, no questions asked, Shaver thought. It was one method with guaranteed results.

Vostik hung back in the group of pedestrians crossing Burrard. He feared that there was little chance of him getting into the hotel. He was breathing heavily, his clothing was soaked in sweat, and it was impossible to conceal his agitation. A police officer was bound to notice and stop him for questioning.

He had almost decided to retreat back across the street to a pay phone when McDermott's cruiser approached with its siren wailing. Instinctively, Vostik pushed ahead boldly now, the phone call to the lookout forgotten, his mind focused again on catching Shaver.

McDermott pulled up in front of the Georgia Street entrance with Vostik running along the sidewalk behind him. The constable supposedly keeping a watch on persons using the door failed to notice the colonel slip into the hotel. All his attention was on McDermott.

At this same moment, McDermott's radio-telephone rang with a call placed by Benson, who had given up trying to reach the inspector on his police radio. McDermott hesitated, wondering whether or not he should answer, and decided not to take the risk. It could be Superintendent Sibley complaining about his go-slow order to the motorcade.

McDermott got out of the car and called the constable over. He questioned him as to whether a drunk in a stolen car had been taken into custody recently in the vicinity of the hotel. The officer replied that some sort of arrest had been made around the corner on Burrard. McDermott decided he should check there first before going into the hotel.

Shaver took a deep breath to compose himself and then marched purposefully across the lobby to the elevators. He had pulled on only the bare necessities – the motorcycle officer's cap, rain slicker, and knee boots – but they were all he needed for acceptance. The police he passed merely nodded in perfunctory recognition of the uniform.

Just a few steps more, Shaver thought, starting to relax, and then he saw Vostik coming toward him. The colonel recognized him at the same time and both froze.

Shaver almost made the mistake of pulling the rifle from his shoulder and then he realized that Vostik had just as much to lose as he had from a gun battle at this point. It would be suicide for the colonel to fire at him now. He wouldn't dare do it. Not in a crowded hotel lobby. Not with police on all sides. Or would he . . . ?

It was worth the gamble, Shaver told himself, bolting for the nearest elevator. He bullied aboard in front of the waiting passengers and then swung around and blocked their entry. 'Emergency, don't wait,' he ordered the operator. 'Take it up. Now!'

The girl obeyed without question and the door closed as Vostik came lurching through the milling passengers. 'What floor . . . ?'

'Just up, damn you,' Shaver shouted.

The girl started the car, but the strong smell of liquor warned her something was wrong. She turned to look and let out a piercing scream.

Shaver flicked the rifle butt against her jaw and took over the controls as she dropped to the floor. He wondered what had set her off – the whiskey smell? bloodshot eyes? slurred speech? – and then saw the splatters of blood on the carpet. His blood.

That snapped it, Shaver thought. He had probably left a trail leading back to the assistant manager's office. It would be noticed soon, and then the two unconscious policemen would be found, and then he'd have everybody after his hide. Vostik plus every trigger-happy cop in the building.

Shaver cursed his decision to take the elevator instead of the stairs. It was only semi-automatic and wouldn't move without an operator. The indicator in the lobby would be a finger pointing remorselessly. Vostik would know where to come hunting and so would the police and both would be shooting to kill. He'd be marked as a maniac the moment he sprayed the street with gunfire to head off Kosygin's motorcade.

Even though he was wasting precious seconds, Shaver took the elevator to the top floor, thinking that the higher he went, the longer he kept Vostik waiting in the lobby. The colonel had no choice but to stay put until the indicator stopped.

The ride up seemed to take forever, and when the car finally reached its destination Shaver burst out blindly. Had he paused to look, he would have seen that another elevator was coming directly to the top floor, bypassing all the others. But Shaver's only thought was to get to the end of the corridor. To kick out the window, aim into the street, fire . . .

In the other elevator, Vostik was smiling tensely at the operator, who had accepted his credentials at face value, and who thought it was very exciting to be rushing a sweat-lathered KGB officer to an important meeting. Like Shaver, the colonel also had only one objective now. He had to get to the room where the lookout was radioing instructions to the helicopter. He had to stop the assassination.

Vostik told himself he had no other choice. He hadn't dared wait in the lobby until he knew Shaver's destination. By the time he did that, Shaver would have accomplished his purpose, which obviously was to create havoc by firing into the street, and then it was a tossup as to who reached him first and whether or not he lived or died. And if Shaver lived and told his story and had Kosygin's shattered body as proof?

No, Vostik thought. That wasn't going to happen. The helicopter would be turned back. The radio transmitter would be hurriedly smuggled out of the hotel. Nothing would be left to support a wild tale of the KGB's involvement in a supposed assassination that hadn't even been attempted . . .

The elevator door opened and Vostik murmured his thanks and stepped out. He started down the corridor and then stopped abruptly. What were those spots on the carpet? Blood?

McDermott was oblivious to Benson's page as he dashed madly across the hotel lobby to the motor vehicle entrance. He had to get out onto the street and flag down the motorcade. He had to keep it out of rifle range.

Shaver had gone completely insane, McDermott thought. There was no other explanation. What else would possess him to attack two police officers? Run off with a high powered rifle . . . commandeer an elevator . . .

McDermott plunged out of the door into the arms of a burly KGB security guard. There was a brief violent struggle which the larger man won. His ham fist raised a knot the size of a walnut on McDermott's forehead.

An RCMP sergeant pushed into the fray too late. All he could do was inform the KGB guard of his mistake. 'For Christ's sake. That's one of *our* blokes.'

The KGB man shrugged helplessly. 'How was I to know? He was running like a maniac. He fought with me. I thought . . .'

'Forget it,' the sergeant said. He wondered why the inspector had been running. Where was he headed? And what was he trying to do?

'I'm sorry.'

'It's all right,' the sergeant said. He thought it would be a while before he had his questions answered. The inspector was out colder than yesterday's duck.

Shaver used the rifle butt twice more when he reached the door opening out onto the roof of the hotel. The first blow cut down the hapless police officer lounging against it. The second smashed the lock open.

Once outside, Shaver saw with satisfaction that he had been correct in changing his plans. The peaked roof dropped away at a sharp angle, far too steep and slippery to risk posting guards here, so he had passed his last hurdle at the door. Below him – an abrupt drop of some thirty feet – a jumble of dormers and turrets jutted out along the lower slopes of the roof. There were dozens of places to hide and he could hold off an army from their dark crevices. He wasn't going to be trapped like a rat in a dead-end corridor. He wasn't going to be shot down before he had a chance to explain. Hell, no – he was going to dig in, and he was going to defend himself, and he was going to force them to negotiate a truce and listen to his story.

Slinging the rifle over his shoulder, Shaver cautiously worked his way along the ridge, glad to be drunk and beyond fear. Had he been sober, he would have turned back. Not only could a slight misstep send him plunging to his doom, but he was out in the open and bathed in spotlights illuminating the roof, an easy target for the police marksmen posted atop neighboring buildings. He could only pray that none would glance his way until he made it to a protected position from which to fire into the street.

He reached the end of the ridge and slipped over the side onto the west slope and hung there trying to decide. There were several suitable places and he might as well take an extra moment to choose the best. His life could depend on it.

Shaver agonized over his decision and finally settled on a cluster of centrally located dormers. He braced himself for the long slide down the roof's metal sheathing and was just about to let go when he heard the helicopter. It was very close by the sound of it. Two or three blocks away at most.

Vostik's kamikaze pilot?

He'd soon know, Shaver thought, changing his plans once again, and then he heard a second helicopter approaching. It was farther away. Coming from a different direction. Barely audible.

Shaver twisted around trying to get a sighting and found himself staring into Vostik's pistol. He ducked too late and there was a muffled bang as a red flash exploded in his brain. The rush of hot blood blinded him and he could feel himself starting to slide down the roof. He was gaining momentum . . . going faster and faster . . .

Vostik leaned forward eagerly. This he had to witness. Shaver sliding inexorably to the edge of the roof. Tumbling over the eaves trough. Plunging into space . . .

'Aiyee!' Vostik screamed, losing his footing. He flung the pistol away and grabbed for the ridge, but it was out of reach. He started to slide down in Shaver's wake.

Shaver slammed painfully against a dormer peak. He rolled off to one side, headed for certain death, and then his fall was stopped abruptly, the slicker catching on a jagged edge of flashing. A wild scream roused him from his stupor and he wiped the blood out of his eyes and saw Vostik sliding by.

'Please,' Vostik cried, his stump outstretched, groping with invisible fingers. 'In the name of God . . .'

Shaver thought that the colonel must be very stupid. It would be easy enough for him to stop sliding. All he had to do was turn in his toes and stiffen his body and hold as still as possible. But he'd never stop if he kept thrashing around in a wild panic. He'd just keep sliding if he did that. Down and down he'd go. Closer and closer to the edge.

'Please,' Vostik begged.

Shaver grinned drunkenly and blew him a kiss good-by.

Nineteen

The KGB agent radioing instructions to the helicopter quickly recovered from the shock of seeing a body plunge past his window. If Colonel Vostik was half as smart as he professed, he would have planned for this to happen, the agent thought. Imagine someone falling from the roof at such an opportune moment! What could be more perfect?

Kosygin's motorcade was less than half a block away. The helicopter was precisely positioned. One of the most significant political assassinations in modern times was about to take place – and no one was watching either the motorcade or the helicopter. Instead, they were all staring at that pitiful lump on the sidewalk, fascinated by the crumpled corpse of a security guard who had been stupid enough to venture onto the hotel's treacherous roof.

It had to be a guard, and a Russian at that, probably. Would a Canadian take such a risk for Kosygin? The agent smiled at the thought of a Russian corpse – it meant one less execution in the bloodbath that would follow the Premier's death – and then radioed his last order to the helicopter. 'Ten seconds, Fat Boy. Start your dive.'

Immediately above him on the roof, Shaver was still hanging precariously by the snagged rain slicker, a bloodied caricature of a drunk suffering double vision. He knew there was only one police department helicopter – yet he could see *two* of them.

He had to make an immediate decision – if he waited for them to get closer it would be too late – but there was no rational basis for choosing. They appeared identical in every respect. It was too dark to see inside the plastic bubbles.

His mind screamed with the question. Which was real and which was fake? Which bore the kamikaze?

Shaver blasphemed – only a depraved God would offer an

impossible choice – and then his crazed frustration drove him to an impossible solution. He wouldn't choose between them. He'd riddle both.

His mind made up, Shaver took careful aim at the plastic bubble of the closest helicopter, which was swooping in from the southeast, a searchlight stabbing along the rooftops of the buildings in its path. He squeezed off four shots in rapid succession and the machine began to shudder violently. Without waiting to see the final result, Shaver swung about and sighted in on the second chopper, hovering almost a block to the north. He again fired four quick shots but nothing happened.

Was it too far away? Shaver wondered. He glanced to his left and saw that the first helicopter was wobbling down onto Robsonstrasse like a wounded bird. If it exploded – *really* exploded – that would settle the question, and it was lucky he had missed with his second burst, he thought. He waited for the blast and there was a muffled crash instead and when he looked back the other chopper had disappeared.

'God, no,' Shaver whispered. He had downed the wrong machine. The other one was in a power dive now, its engine roaring at full pitch, and it was already cutting down behind the Burrard Building, headed straight for the motorcade.

Shaver swung the rifle around and waited in hopeless resignation. He knew where it would reappear, but firing would be a useless gesture, because not even a cannon could deter the damn thing then. Sheer momentum would take it the short distance remaining.

The crowd broke in panic as the chopper came swooping over the parking lot. Kosygin's limousine was forced to a dead halt in the center of a screaming mass of people. Escape was impossible.

Then, inexplicably, the pilot suddenly reversed and banked, as if he had decided to stop and put on a show. A fat figure appeared at the door of the plastic bubble. He leaned forward with his arms outstretched. There was the look of a savior about him – a man prepared to die for a cause.

Of course, Shaver thought. That bloated pig was Henke, and while he might be too drugged to realize it, he was putting on a show, all right. There was a movie camera grinding away somewhere, and the film was destined to find its way to a newspaper. Photographic proof that a Russian-hating CIA sex pervert had sacrificed himself to kill Kosygin. Hadn't you heard? The camera never lies.

Shaver squeezed the trigger and kept firing until the whole rifle clip was exhausted. The plastic bubble shattered in a dozen places and the helicopter spun around violently while the mortally wounded pilot vainly fought for control. Then it dropped like a stone into the middle of the parking lot.

Henke was thrown clear by the impact. Miraculously – or was it because the drug had made him so relaxed and fearless? – he escaped with nothing worse than a few severe bruises. He struggled to his feet and staggered across the parking lot toward the hotel.

Samuel squeezed out of the wreckage and crawled painfully after him. There was a plunger, a timing device, that he desperately wanted to push, because even from this distance the explosives were powerful enough to kill Kosygin.

He *had* to reach it – but he couldn't.

Mueller scrambled down off the truck and ran to his stricken compatriot.

'The plunger,' Samuel gasped. 'The plunger ... push it ...'

Mueller left him to die and ran back to Henke, who had stumbled out into the street, sagging under the weight of the explosives. Police were closing in on him warily.

'Be careful!' Mueller shouted. 'There's a plunger. Don't touch it.'

A grim-faced officer nodded his thanks and signaled to the others closing in. This was going to be done properly. No mistakes.

Twenty

Shaver pulled off his cap and waited for his eyes to adjust to the gloom of The Stump Club. Yes, the dirty old fart was at his table, as per usual. There were some things that never changed.

'Come on,' Shaver said. He took Bogna by the hand and led her across the floor. 'Mind if we join you?'

Petapiece looked up from his newspaper in shocked surprise. Shaver was the last man he had ever wanted to see again. 'W-where did you come from?'

'The VD Clinic,' Shaver said, pulling out a chair for Bogna. 'Blood tests. We're thinking of getting married.'

'M-married?' Petapiece stammered, making it sound unthinkable.

'She's got mileage left,' Shaver said defensively.

'Well, that's a surprise,' Petapiece answered, becoming more and more flustered. He thought that he was going to be stomped to death any moment now – and he'd only just recovered from the previous attack.

'We thought you should be the first to know,' Bogna explained.

'That's right,' Shaver said, holding her hand. 'Until you saddled me with that Henke business, I never knew how much . . .' His voice trailed off as the color rose to his cheeks. 'The credit is yours, is all.'

Petapiece finally realized that he wasn't going to be killed. 'You mean I'm the matchmaker?'

'Yes.'

'Well,' Petapiece said, starting to breathe again. 'Well . . .' He fumbled with his newspaper. 'All's well that ends well.'

'You've been reading about him?' Bogna asked, adoring eyes on her betrothed. The bullet crease along his skull made him all the more handsome.

'As a matter of fact, yes,' Petapiece admitted. He put the paper aside and smiled tentatively at Shaver. 'So you kept your stripes, eh, lad? And got a bright shiny medal to boot?'

'Lady Luck's work,' Shaver told him. 'It would have been jail instead had any coppers died.' He patted around for his cigarettes. 'How about you?'

'Me?' Petapiece laughed. 'Oh, they're still trying to think of something suitable, I guess.'

'Newfoundland?'

'Doubtless.'

They both laughed and Bogna joined in, marveling at how drastically her life had changed. She still didn't get Shaver's jokes. But now they were funny.

'Marriage,' Petapiece enthused. He looked from Shaver to Bogna and rubbed his grimy hands together. 'This calls for a drink.'

'A drink,' Shaver agreed.

'A drink,' said Bogna.

Shaver got out his Sweet Caps. He'd wait forever, he thought. But diddily damned if he'd buy.